TO CATCH A RAINBOW

TO CATCH A RAINBOW

ESTELLE THOMPSON

WALKER AND COMPANY
NEW YORK

7 4163

ML '80 0 3 1 1 9

First published in the United States of America
in 1980 by the Walker Publishing Company, Inc.

ISBN: 0-8027-0652-5

Library of Congress Catalog Card Number: 80-7564

Printed in the United States of America

10 9 8 7 6 5 4 3 2 1

ACKNOWLEDGEMENTS

A number of people have helped me in various ways in the writing of this story. Some have assisted with research into events and customs of the period. Some have told me true stories of incidents in the lives of pioneering relatives — stories which have been handed down through several generations and have been woven, in some cases, into the action of this book. Others have given valuable authoritative advice on aboriginal customs. All have given me much-valued encouragement.

My grateful thanks go to Mollie Krebs, Camilla and Les Alcorn, Isabel and Harold Thornell, Roy Kilpatrick and Bernadette Harris.

Estelle Thompson.

One

There were white gables and a leafy lane, and it was spring.

It was always spring when she remembered it. She wondered why the memory had to come with such force just now, and she shut her eyes so that the man beside her wouldn't see the pain in them.

She needn't have worried. He had eyes only for the scene before them, oblivious of the rain that beat down in heavy monotony, streaming off his wide felt hat.

"Look at it, Elizabeth!"

She glanced up at him as he sat beside the driver, and the warm rain of a Queensland February summer beat in her face. She had long since given up trying to keep dry, though the children, huddled farther back under the canvas cover, were fairly well sheltered.

The driver had stopped the covered dray on a rise above the river and Robert was looking out over the packed straggle of habitation, his keen dark face alight with excitement.

"Think of it! There's a fortune to be made here with nothing but a pick and shovel. Gold by the bucketful!"

She looked at this raw town that had hurtled into being in the frenzied wake of that one magical, terrible word: gold.

She saw a street of pit-sawn, shingle-roofed buildings –

stores, hotels – with their signs brave in the wilderness. She saw slab huts and bark humpies and tents pitched along the gullies and over the hills like myriad scraps of paper blown helter-skelter by the wind: piled up thickly here, sparse there. There were countless windlass-rigs and mounds of earth that told of mine-shafts burrowing into the earth in quest of the fickle dream-metal.

There were great poppet-heads and mulloch heaps of the deep reef-mines, where machinery and big business had moved into the areas the individual picks and shovels could no longer utilize, and the growl of the crushers endlessly muttered over the town.

And everywhere – everywhere – was mud. Ankle-deep, knee-deep, putting the final seal on the utter ugliness.

And the trees that were still standing streamed rain, dispiritedly, as if they mourned their slashed-down comrades and the savaging of their habitat.

The taciturn driver clicked his tongue and his two horses plodded down the slope. A bearded gnome of a man, he had been at the wharf in Maryborough when the coastal steamer had tied up.

Elizabeth had been longing to get off the crowded boat, jammed as it was with fortune-hunters of many kinds and cargo to supply the needs of the miners already on the field. This was the easiest route to the new gold-field: the steamer from Brisbane to Maryborough, and then by road to the Gympie field – by coach, if you were lucky enough to get a seat, or had the fare for it.

In the crowd on the wharf, Robert hadn't been lucky enough to get seats on the coach, but he'd seen the man with the dray and asked for a lift for his family. The man had eyed Elizabeth and the two children.

"No way for a lady to travel," he growled. "Let alone nippers."

"But plenty of these people are going to walk it!" Robert had protested, nodding at the crowd disembarking.

"Plenty of people," the dray owner had grunted, "are mad." He had taken a pipe from his mouth, looked over Robert's neat clothes and nodded. "Aye," was all he'd said, and loaded the Waldens' luggage into his dray.

It had rained steadily all the way, and they had spent a wretched night huddled under the tarpaulin with the dray bogged at a creek-crossing. Elizabeth wondered why she had ever thought the boat uncomfortable.

Now she stared at the diggings: this crude town that had saved the infant colony of Queensland from ruin following the Bank crash of 1866 – little more than two years before – and lured restless men from all over the country and beyond, just as it had lured Robert Walden to throw away his Sydney business venture just when it looked as if it was set for solid success, and head north, dazzled by the wild stories of James Nash's discovery and the fortunes that could be won.

Some of the stories were even true.

As his horses bent their heads into the driving rain, the dray-driver shifted his pipe from one corner of his mouth to the other and said drily to Robert, "And where are you fixin' to live till you dig up your first bucketful of gold?"

"I'll get a cabin built once I've staked my claim," Robert said cheerfully.

"Meanwhile it'll be none too dry under a tree," the driver commented. "Never got no tent, did you?"

"No. Supplies were sold out." Robert grinned, uncrushed. "We'll put up at a hotel for the present. Can you recommend one?"

The dray-driver looked at him for a long time. "There's thirty thousand people on the diggin's, scramblin' here from all directions," he said finally, "an' the man says he'll put up at a hotel. Just like that." He spat expertly over the side of the dray without turning his head.

"You could," he observed, "try Maggie's place."

Before Robert could answer a coach drawn by four fine horses came lumbering towards them, led by a mounted constable. Armed police sat beside the driver and another policeman rode behind.

"The gold escort," the dray-driver grunted.

"The gold escort!" Eight-year-old Edward's voice shrilled from under cover of the tarpaulin as he scrambled forward. "Let me see!"

"Me, too!" his sister cried.

Two tousled heads, one as honey-blond as his mother and the other as dark as her father, peered eagerly out.

"Will there be bushrangers?" Edward demanded. "Will the coach be robbed?"

"'Tain't likely," the dray-driver told him. "But like as not there'd be trouble if the escort weren't armed an' all. There's always them as would rather use a gun than a pick an' shovel."

"No need even to use a pick and shovel, from the stories I've heard in Sydney," Robert said. "They tell of men finding nuggets by the handful, washing river-gravel in a miner's cradle."

"Aye. An' there's plenty found just river-gravel, too. Anyways, you're a mite late for that. Bit late for all the shallow stuff. Alluvial's near gone."

"Gone! But —" Robert looked shocked. "Look, I can see plenty of men down there. Aren't they washing gravel in cradles?" The confidence had come back into his voice.

"Everyone has to wash pay-dirt. Only way to get out the gold. Lot of Chinese down there, too. Patient, the Chinese. Often find what Europeans miss. But I tell you —"

He reined up his horse in front of a shingle-roofed building whose painted sign said "Trent's General Store".

He glanced at Robert's hands and smiled sourly.

"You'll have to dig, mister. That's Maggie's place," he added, jerking his thumb at a two-storeyed weatherboard hotel whose swinging sign read "Wild Swan", and went into the store.

"Wait, children, I'll come back for you," Robert said, jumping down and holding up his arms for his wife and swinging her down to the muddy earth beside him.

She pulled her sodden shawl more closely around her head and they ran through the rain to the comparative shelter of the hotel awning which reached over the earthen footpath. A steady buzz of men's voices came from behind the wooden door with its arctic-glass panel.

Robert pushed open the door and they went into a large saloon-bar full of voices and tobacco smoke and the smell of spirits and damp clothes.

The rumble of voices faded as men saw Elizabeth and one or two seated at scrubbed-pine tables got awkwardly to their feet. A small, lively-looking woman of about forty was serving behind the bar and Robert went across to her.

"Pardon me, but are you the proprietress?"

She paused in what she was doing and looked him over with alert blue eyes.

"I'm Maggie Doyle, yes. What can I do for you?"

The voice was briskly businesslike, the accent strongly Cockney.

"I'd like rooms for my wife and myself and two children."

Maggie Doyle's gaze went beyond him to the woman who stood just inside the door: a tall woman – almost as tall as Robert – whose grey eyes studied the scene in the bar as coolly as she would have checked the setting of her dinner-table at home, her whole attitude one of unshakeable tranquility.

"Gawd love us!" Maggie muttered. "Don't none of you

men 'ave no sense? What d'you think this place is, eh? The west end of London?''

Robert raised his eyebrows. "My wife and children are hardly the first to come to the goldfields. Do you have rooms?''

"No, I do not! There's thirty thousand people, close to, on these diggin's, and they still keep pourin' in. I don't 'ave no spare rooms, I can tell you.''

"I see. Well, can you advise me where else I might try around the town?''

"Nowhere.''

"I beg your pardon?''

"Nowhere, I said! Ain't a place in town with spare rooms.''

Robert rubbed his clipped black moustache uneasily. "But – what am I to do? My family have to have somewhere to stay till I can build us a hut, at least.''

"Shoulda thought of that before, shouldn't you? Buy a tent. Plenty do.''

"Well, I've tried that. It seems there aren't any available.''

"Gawd love us! Ain't that typical? You bleedin' stupid men come bargin' up 'ere without a thought in your thick 'eads but gold.''

Maggie's eyes flicked to Elizabeth again, noting the wet clothes and the honey-blond hair darkened with rain.

"Oh, all right, all right! I'll fix somethin' up. Gawd knows why I bother. Bert, take over 'ere while I show the lady and gentleman upstairs, like a good chap. An' mind you don't go givin' no free drinks to your friends.''

A big man in his early forties with lively dark eyes and a flash of white teeth in a grin that showed behind a bushy black beard came from one of the tables and took up his post behind the bar.

That night after Elizabeth had put out the candle she stood at the sash window staring out through the rain-streaked glass to where, here and there, the glint of a candle or oil-lamp showed.

The wind still blew at nearly gale-force, but the hiss of rain across the shingles was drowned by the noise from the bar, where Maggie banged out tunes on a battered piano while the miners sang in a variety of keys largely dictated by their alcohol intake, and argued, and loudly competed for a favouring smile from one or other of the barmaids who by day doubled as housemaids and of whose after-hours activities presumably Maggie Doyle asked no questions.

From the bed Robert asked, "What are you thinking?"

"Can anyone think with that noise?" she parried lightly.

"Says she, dodging the question," Robert said. "Liz, I know it isn't going to be easy for a while. But it will come out right. It has to. Look, even in the few hours we've been here I've heard enough stories of fortunes made here to convince even you."

She nodded in the darkness. "Oh, I'm sure there are plenty of successes."

He heard the wry note in her voice and said gently, "Look, darling, I know coming here was a gamble for us – it's a gamble for everyone who comes. But surely it's worth it!"

A fight erupted in the saloon and spilled violently into the rain-sodden street.

She turned away from the window. "Yes, I'm sure it is." Suddenly she was cold in the warm night air and she climbed into the bed beside him, grateful for his arms about her, shutting out memories.

Two

Two days later the sky was almost cloudless and the sun poured down sweltering heat tempered a little by an easterly breeze, and sun and breeze between them began to dry up the mud.

Glad to be out of doors to catch some benefit of the breeze, Elizabeth took the children out to walk the still-sodden street and look at the town.

Already Robert had staked his claim and chosen a spot to build a hut, and this morning he had begun work on it. Maggie Doyle had introduced him to Bert Peters, the black-bearded man with the friendly grin who had taken over the bar-work for Maggie while she had shuffled things and people around to make rooms available for the Waldens the day they arrived.

"Bert's a handy-man," Maggie told Robert. "Ain't much he can't turn his hand to. Dare say he knows more about buildin' huts than you'll likely ever learn. You might as well give Captain Walden a 'and as muck around that useless mine of yours, Bert," she added.

She looked at Robert. "Bert an' Dr Miller went into partnership, like," she explained drily. "Dr Miller set Bert up and Bert was to do the work, and they was goin' to share the fortune."

Bert shrugged good-humouredly. "It must have just

missed the reef," he said. "Story of my life, I guess. Ah, well, maybe a man's better off staying poor, from some of the things you see. You're a military man, then, Captain Walden?"

Robert shook his head. "I used to be. Resigned my commission in England to come out to New South Wales."

So, Elizabeth reflected now as she looked along the street that was full of bustle, Robert and Bert Peters were out building a cabin. It was strange, she thought, that Bert, having failed at one attempt to strike gold, seemed to have no wish to try again, but was content to take odd-jobs around the town. But then, even in the wildest gold-rush, there were always men who never felt the burning fever that drove so many.

The children, elated at getting out of doors, seemed quite unconcerned with heat and mud, and absorbed in the activity around them.

It was incredible, Elizabeth thought, how this town – rough though it was – had mushroomed into being.

Less than two years ago these hills had been covered with standing timber. Nothing disturbed the wildlife, except passing groups of aborigines on a hunt. The naked dark men might have startled a wallaby into crashing headlong through the bush, or silenced the cooing of the flocks of pigeons. The only white men who came into the valley of the Mary River were timbergetters in search of cedar, and a scatter of settlers who recognized good farmland.

Then a bearded man named Nash had come with no friend but his dog, and found that a thousand fortunes were there for the taking.

For the lucky ones.

Now there were general stores and blacksmiths, bakers and banks, butchers and hotels. The whine and bite of saws at the sawmill were testimony to the need for more buildings. Here and there a church stood as a reminder that a man might profit little if he gained all the riches of the earth, and lost his soul; though it seemed probable that most would pay attention to the riches first.

Drays and buggies and men on horseback and people on foot hurried purposefully about.

Suddenly Elizabeth stopped. "Wait, children," she said.

Sarah looked up enquiringly. "What is it, Mummy?"

Somewhere down the street, out of sight, Elizabeth could hear men shouting.

"I think it's a fight, Mother," Edward volunteered hopefully. "Shall I go –"

He broke off as a horse came into view, coming at an insane gallop, clearly out of control of its desperately-clinging rider who kept shouting in warning while he fought uselessly to rein the animal in.

People scattered from the street to shelter in doorways. Elizabeth grabbed each of the children by a hand and pulled them back against the wall of a bank building.

"Inside, quickly!" she told them, backing toward the doorway as she watched the bolting horse.

A short, nuggety man in Crimean shirt and moleskin trousers had paused in crossing the street to fill his pipe, apparently blithely unaware of his danger.

Someone – Elizabeth supposed later it must have been her own voice – screamed at him, but he stood with his back to the horse, absently tamping tobacco into the bowl of the pipe, absorbed in watching his dog, which had just chased a rat under the floorboards of Trent's General Store and was now trying to dig it out.

The rider of the bolting horse sawed at the reins, trying to pull the animal away from the man, but the horse was blind with panic.

Afterwards, Elizabeth marvelled at how much seemed to

happen in the tiny fragment of time from the moment she saw the man's danger.

Pushing the children hard against the wall with a terse: "Stay there!", she ran headlong across the horse's path, snatching the man's arm and pulling him with her as she ran for the other side of the street.

She felt the splatter of mud from the crazed animal's hooves and heard its rasping breath somewhere terrifyingly close.

Then it was gone and there was an instant jumble of voices and the sound of someone running.

Shaken, she clung for a moment to the arm of the man she had pulled clear of the horse's path, aware that he was staring at her in bewilderment as she tried to get her breath.

She heard someone say, "Get Dr Miller."

She turned quickly. "No, no – I'm quite unhurt. Just –"

She stopped. Across the muddy street Edward stood where she had left him, but Sarah lay like a crumpled doll while a big fair-haired man knelt beside her, gently turning her over.

"Sarah!" Elizabeth never remembered crossing the street again, but in a moment she was beside the little girl and the man who carefully cradled her head.

"What happened?"

A white-faced Edward said, "The horse bumped her. I hung on to her, Mother, but the horse just ran over us!"

The fair-haired man looked up at Elizabeth. "The animal swerved after almost knocking down you and old Tom, and lunged against the wall. I think the little girl's only stunned. Don't be frightened. Someone's gone to fetch Dr Miller."

Elizabeth was dimly aware of people around her, but she saw only the stillness of her daughter.

Someone said, "Let's carry her inside, John."

The fair-haired man had pulled off his coat and folded it carefully under Sarah's head.

"No!" he said sharply. "Wait till the doctor's had a look at her. If she has broken bones we may only hurt her more by moving her."

"Let's hope Dr Miller's sober," a woman's voice said.

"Sufficiently sober to cope with this, madam," a deep voice said cheerfully. "Now, then, what's happened?"

A short, stocky man with no hat on his thinning grey hair knelt beside Sarah and began to run careful hands over her in a clearly practised manner, apparently paying not the slightest attention to the confusion of detail provided by a dozen bystanders.

Presently he said, "What remarkable human being had the good sense to leave her where she was, by the way? Oh," he added as he looked up. "You, John, I gather. Well, as it happens I don't think there's any real damage done."

He looked at Elizabeth with kind blue eyes behind gold-rimmed glasses. "You're her mother, madam?"

Elizabeth nodded. "But Doctor, she's so – so pale and still –"

He smiled. "Knocked out. But I don't think it's any worse than that. She's beginning to come around now."

Sarah stirred slightly and in a few moments opened her eyes with a puzzled whimper. As Elizabeth spoke to her reassuringly she sat up, put her arms around her mother's neck and began to cry.

Dr Miller nodded approvingly and stood up. "Where do you live, madam? I'll carry the child to your house."

"We're staying at the 'Wild Swan'," Elizabeth told him. "Thank you, Doctor, but I can carry her. It's such a short way."

She paused as the tall man who had gone first to Sarah's

aid stooped down to pick up his coat. "Oh, your coat!" she said. "It's covered in mud. Please let me take it and clean it for you."

His blue eyes met hers in a slow smile. "You have the little girl to care for. Don't worry about my coat." He held her gaze for a second, and then added almost awkwardly, "What you just did was a very brave thing. You very likely saved old Tom's life."

Maggie Doyle brought extra blankets and helped Elizabeth put Sarah to bed. Dr Miller watched the child carefully for a while and finally nodded and got up to go.

"Put cold wet cloths on her head and keep her quiet for the rest of the day," he said. "She'll probably want to sleep a lot, so let her. Good for her. There's no sign of any real concussion. A lump on the head and a few bruises, that's all. She'll be as lively as ever by tomorrow. The horse must have just grazed her."

Elizabeth shivered. "I shouldn't have left the children. But I couldn't just stand there and see that old man knocked down. Doctor," she added, raising her eyes from Sarah, "who was that man?"

He smiled. "Old Tom Sanderson. He's not so old, either – only in his fifties. But he's as deaf as any post. That's why he took no notice of the horse and all the commotion: he's not stupid, he just didn't know there *was* any commotion. Apparently he'd always been deaf in one ear. Worked a claim here with a partner, and one day he was at the bottom of the shaft and his mate was on the windlass winding up the buckets as Tom filled 'em with dirt, and the windlass-rope snapped and the bucket fell down the shaft and hit Tom on the head. It should've killed him, but it didn't – just destroyed the eardrum in his good ear and left him stone deaf."

Elizabeth shook her head. "Oh, I see. But I didn't mean that man — I meant the fair-haired man who wouldn't let anyone move Sarah till you came."

"Oh, you mean John Trent? Owns a big general store. Good fellow, John. Solid as a rock. See you keep her warm," he added as he went out. "It may seem a hot day to you, but she's suffering shock."

Maggie Doyle saw him out and came back.

"Proper gentleman, the doctor is," she told Elizabeth. "Drinks like a fish, but a proper gentleman. You won't never find a better doctor, neither, when he's sober. One of the fashionable doctors in London, 'e was — *and* deserved to be."

"This," Elizabeth said wryly, dipping the towel again in the bowl of water and putting it gently back on Sarah's bruised head, "seems a strange place to find one of London's fashionable doctors."

"Brandy," Maggie said promptly. "Can't leave it alone. Won't never hold no regular practice. Can't. So he has to follow around places like this, where people are glad of any doctor. An' like I say, there's none better when he's sober, an' he ain't so bad when he's drunk, either, if it's just something ordinary. I've seen him set a broken leg straight as a die when he was so drunk he had to do it sittin' on a chair 'cause he couldn't stand. I'll go an' make you some tea," she added. "You look like you could use it."

She was back in a minute, followed by a mud-spattered man who carried a felt hat twisted nervously in his rough hands

"Someone to see you, Mrs Walden," Maggie announced. "It's the man whose horse bumped little Sarah."

"Is she all right, Mrs Walden?" the man asked anxiously. "I came as fast as I could. I had to ask around to find out who you were, and everything. Is she all right?"

"The doctor says she'll be fine by tomorrow," Elizabeth

reassured him. "She was only knocked out. Probably the horse pushed her back against the wall."

The man wiped a hand across a sweating forehead. "I thought he'd killed her."

"Yes," Elizabeth said, looking at Sarah. "So did I."

She looked up. "You were fortunate not to be injured yourself. What made the horse bolt like that?"

"My pack-horse had pulled away from me, and I was taking a short-cut through the bush to head him off, and I rode Gunpowder – my saddle-horse – slam into a clump of gympies. He just went mad."

"Gympies?" Elizabeth sounded puzzled.

"The stinging-tree. The town is named after it. It has furry dull green leaves, and if you touch them they set up a fearful stinging burn in your skin that's nearly unbearable. It'll keep on stinging for weeks, every time you have a wash. Water must push the little furry spines off the leaves deeper into your skin or something. Gunpowder just went crazy." He shook his head, still looking shocked. "Crazy."

Elizabeth shuddered. "How horrible! Is your horse calmed down now?"

"Yes," the man said tightly. "He's real calm. He hit into an awning-post up the street and broke his shoulder. I had to shoot him. Best horse I ever had," he added in a voice that blurred a little, and he turned quickly away and went.

Maggie Doyle came in with tea on a tray and looked keenly at Elizabeth, who was staring, pale and tense, after the man who had just left.

" 'Ere, what's all this, then?" Maggie demanded. "I meet that bloke on the stairs all tears, an' I come in 'ere an' find you lookin' like somethin' the cat wouldn't even bother to drag home."

Elizabeth leapt to her feet, her hands over her face, and turned away from Sarah's bed.

"I hate it!" she said, and although she kept her voice low

it was close to hysteria. "I hate this town, I hate this country!"

She wheeled on Maggie. "What fiendish sort of place is it where even a plant can drive an animal so insane it kills itself? Where men will live in hovels just so they may search for gold they will probably never find? I wish to Heaven we had never found the accursed country, let alone its gold! I can't –"

Her voice broke, choking on a sob.

She turned to the window and stood for a minute as if she were looking down on the street. But her hands at her sides were clenched into fists and her eyes were closed. Presently she turned.

"I'm sorry," she said quietly. "I do beg your pardon for creating a scene. I don't usually."

Maggie's sharp blue eyes studied her for a moment, and then she gave a little nod, as if she had come to a decision.

She looked at Edward, hovering uncertainly near his sister's bed. "Right, then, young man, I want to talk to your mother a minute, so you stay here an' look after your little sister. Right?"

"No, no!" Elizabeth protested quickly. "I mustn't leave her."

"Stuff and nonsense! She's all right. Big brother'll look after her. Just sit beside her," she told Edward. "You might read to her outa one of them books of yours. I've heard your mother teachin' you to read, haven't I? A nice bit of plum cake to cheer you up, and a bit for Sarah, too. There's nothing wrong with her stomach," she added as Elizabeth began to protest. "Right?" she asked Edward.

His grey eyes lit at the sight of the plum cake and he nodded. "Yes, *please*, Mrs Doyle."

Maggie laughed and ruffled his hair. "Right. Come along with me, Mrs Walden," she ordered, picking up the tea-tray and striding out into the hall. Elizabeth, with an anxious glance back at Sarah, who was sitting up demurely eating her cake in spite of her paleness, found herself meekly following.

Maggie hurried down the hallway to a door marked: "Private. Keep out", balanced the tray in one hand while she took a key from her apron pocket with the other, opened the door and motioned Elizabeth inside.

Elizabeth stepped into the room and halted in astonishment as Maggie locked the door behind them.

The walls were unpainted as they were in all the other rooms, and the sash window looked down on the same harsh town of raw earth and crude buildings. But there the similarity to other rooms ended. This was an English drawing-room.

A crimson carpet lay on the rough pine floor-boards and long velvet curtains draped the window. A polished oak table was clustered with matching dining chairs, and gracious easy chairs and an elegant sofa were upholstered in brocade. There was fine china and crystal, and one or two good paintings on the walls. Against a wall lined with shelves of books was a small grand piano.

While Elizabeth stared in disbelief, Maggie put down the tea-tray on a small table by the sofa.

"Please sit down, my dear," she said.

It took a moment for the changed tone of voice to register, and then Elizabeth turned swiftly to look at her. The Cockney accent was gone, the voice clear and soft. Even the woman's bearing seemed changed.

She looked at Elizabeth with twinkling eyes and a slightly rueful smile.

"Allow me to introduce Lady Margaret Doyle," she said. "But she, as a daughter of an Earl and the widow of Sir Rupert Doyle, could hardly run a goldfields pub, could she? Or, if she tried, no one would come within shouting distance."

Elizabeth shook her head as if to clear it. "But – why?"

"Why would I be running a goldfields pub? To survive, Mrs Walden. To survive."

She poured tea and handed it.

"My husband, like yours, saw opportunity in the new colonies. We were in comfortable financial circumstances and he established himself quickly in business in Brisbane. His business expanded rapidly – much too rapidly for security. A new venture, for which he heavily borrowed capital, was dependent for success on the building of the new railway from Ipswich to the Darling Downs."

She paused. "Then in 1866 came trouble. There was a drought. There was a financial crisis in England which had to have repercussions here. The price of wool fell. And the Bank crash came. They abandoned the railway because there was no money to go on building it. So my husband was ruined."

She sipped tea, but her thoughts were obviously far away as she put down her cup.

"My husband confused financial ruin with defeat," she said, and added softly, "poor man. One night while I was asleep he took his pistol, went outside, and killed himself."

There was a long stillness. Elizabeth said gently, "I'm sorry."

Margaret Doyle raised her head from studying her hands in her lap.

"I was better off than many," she said. "The colony was in an ugly state in those days. The men who'd been working on the railway were put off, and there was no work for them and they had nothing. If they didn't steal – or couldn't steal – they went hungry. At least I was able to salvage this."

She gestured at the furnishings. "All that's left of the

great dream of the new life in the colonies. Not very impressive, is it? But it's a great deal more than some had. And I got a job as a housemaid."

"Housemaid!" Elizabeth gasped.

Lady Margaret smiled grimly. "I preferred that to a genteel death by starvation. Then the Government offered a reward for the discovery of gold, and there was a rush to go prospecting. They found gold at Nanango and I borrowed a little money from friends and went there to set up a hotel. The only thing," she added, "that isn't a gamble on a goldfield is a hotel, because the one thing you can be sure of is miners' thirst. And loneliness − a sense of being lost, especially once the gloss begins to wear off their hopes."

"That field − Nanango − where is it?"

"Not far from here, really. But it didn't last. It was only a small field. Then Nash found gold here. The odd thing was that they say some cedar-getters had found gold here earlier, but didn't set any store by their find and just went on after the timber they'd come for."

"What about the natives?" Elizabeth asked suddenly. "They must have lived here almost since time began. Isn't it strange they didn't find the gold?"

Margaret shook her head. "Our dark men never worked metal and never had any interest in gold."

"Wise dark men," Elizabeth said.

Margaret shot her a look. "The aborigines have lived here no one knows how many thousands of years. They've never tried to change the land to suit them − only tried to adapt themselves to suit the land. That may well be right. But white men aren't made to think like that, and nothing will change that. They have to adventure, they must have change. It may be right, it may be wrong, but it is fact. We are never content. That's our blessing and our curse. We always want change."

"Not all of us," Elizabeth said, and there was bitterness under the words.

"You think we'd have been better off if the gold had stayed in the ground? Oh, no, my dear. This colony was facing ruin, until the gold was found. With the financial crash, people were hungry. Hungry people are dangerous. Brisbane was an ugly place to be in, at times. There was talk of civil war, and they set up field guns in front of Government House, in case the anger of the hungry got out of official control. If ever a country needed a gold-strike, Queensland needed this one. Once I could see this was going to be a solid field, I came here."

"But why," Elizabeth asked after a moment, "did you try to set up a hotel in the first place? You say you borrowed a little money from friends. Why ever didn't you spend that to buy a passage home? Back to your family?"

"Would you have done that?"

"Yes," Elizabeth said simply. She smiled. "I'm not adventurous, you see. I loved the ordered life I led in England. Even the most ordered life has challenges and triumphs and disasters enough for me. I don't have your strength of character."

Margaret Doyle studied her with candid blue eyes. "I wonder. Strength comes in many guises."

She stood up and walked over to the window. "Unless you were strong, you would never have married Robert Walden. And he would never have married you."

Elizabeth's head came up sharply. "What do you mean?"

"He needs your strength. He always will."

"You're wrong, quite wrong!" Elizabeth was staring at her in astonishment. "Strength! Robert has enough for ten men, and more courage in one finger than I'll muster in a lifetime. Why, he had a distinguished army career, and he's the one who must always be seeking change, chasing adventure."

"Oh, yes." Lady Doyle nodded, almost dreamily. "Bold men are building this country. Their names will be written in history books. But it's the strength of the women that lays the foundations. I've seen your husband playing cards, Mrs Walden. I've seen it sometimes in other men. It gets a grip on them the way drink seizes hold of some men."

She stopped abruptly and turned to look at Elizabeth. "I beg your pardon. I'm intruding in your affairs. Incidentally, no human being but you has ever set foot in this room," she said. "No one knows who I am – no one. Not even –" She brushed a thread from her skirt. "No one. And no one must, not even your husband."

Elizabeth nodded. "Of course."

Margaret Doyle's eyes ran around the room. "The masquerade isn't always easy. This room is my refuge." She smiled faintly.

"Thank you for letting me share it."

Lady Doyle ran a gentle finger along the polished top of the piano. "This country killed my husband. I swore then that it would never beat me. I'll take it on – head on – and I'll beat it on its own terms. And so will you."

Elizabeth stood up to go. "I wish I were as sure of that. But thank you. I must get back to the children –" She broke off at a sudden sound of voices raised angrily in the bar below. "What's that?"

Margaret Doyle was already at the door.

"A right proper old dust-up, or me name's not Maggie Doyle."

She ran for the stairs, Elizabeth, close behind her, urging anxiously, "Be careful! You're not going down there?"

Sounds of fighting and overturned chairs mixed with shouts.

"My bleedin' oath I am!" Maggie flung back. "No bunch of rough-necks is goin' to wreck my place. Now, then, stop this, you bleedin' idiots!" she shouted as she ran down the stairs.

"Jack Fletcher!" she cried out. "Drop that! Drop it, you hear me?"

Fear was sharp in her voice, and the bar was suddenly almost quiet, except for the scraping of hurried boots on the floor as other men moved quickly away from the fighters. But there was menace in the sudden lessening of sound, and as Elizabeth reached the head of the stairs she saw why.

A big man stood with his back to the bar, facing two men who stood about three paces from him, hatred intent in their faces. One of them, a smallish grimy man, had a knife gripped purposefully.

In answer to Maggie Doyle's order to drop it, he said softly, "He jumped our claim. Low rat went down in the night, just as we bottomed on gold. He took out – how much? How much, eh?"

The big man was breathing hard. "Hardly any. That's the truth! All right, I admit I took some. But it's all there, every ounce of it, in that bag I gave you!"

"Liar. I'll cut your throat." He moved a half-step closer.

The big man, never taking his eyes off Fletcher, reached behind him to a whisky bottle on the bar. He lifted it by the neck and with a quick jerk of his wrist smashed it on the edge of the bar, so that he was left holding a weapon of jagged glass almost as fearful if not quite as deadly as the knife in Fletcher's hand.

Maggie's eyes flicked from one to the other and she swallowed quickly as if her throat was suddenly dry.

"Now, then, Jack Fletcher, that'll be enough." Her voice was steady, almost joking in tone. "Come on. 'E's told you you've got all the gold back. That just might be true, you know. Anyway, what've we got ruddy policemen for? Let them settle it. Give me the knife."

She stepped forward and Jack Fletcher snarled without looking at her, "Get back, Maggie, or I'll cut your throat first just for practice."

A man stepped quickly out of the crowd and grabbed her arm. "He means it, Maggie."

"You bleedin' fool, Jack Fletcher!" Maggie flung at the little miner. "You always did have a filthy temper, even sober. And you're drunk!"

Elizabeth backed quietly away from the head of the stairs, anxious not to attract anyone's attention. She saw Maggie glance up, and she saw scorn in the other woman's eyes – whether for her retreat from the ugly scene, for the miner with the knife and his partner standing menacingly beside him, or for the other men afraid to intervene, she didn't know.

Once out of sight of the bar she whirled and ran to the room she and Robert shared. She pulled up the single Austrian bent chair to the wardrobe and climbed on it. On top of the wardrobe, wrapped in canvas, was Robert's fine new American Remington rifle.

She snatched it down, unwrapped and loaded it with hands clumsied by haste, then turned to see Edward, wide-eyed in the doorway.

"Mother! What is –"

She put a finger to her lips. "Stay with Sarah," she said. "No matter what you hear, just stay."

"Is it a hold-up?" Edward whispered, enthralled.

"No. A fight." His mother was already running down the passageway.

She stopped at the head of the stairs. No one noticed her. In the unreal silence in the saloon Jack Fletcher, his partner beside him, had manoeuvred the thief away from the bar.

They circled carefully, Fletcher weaving and feinting, waiting for an opening to get in a knife-thrust and evade the mutilating edge of the broken bottle.

Elizabeth raised the rifle to her shoulder, steadied it against the corner of the wall, and fired.

The bullet smashed into the floorboards between Fletcher and the gold-thief.

Elizabeth worked the rifle bolt, aware of the faces raised to stare at her, aware that the protagonists had frozen in mid-movement. She levelled the rifle at Fletcher.

"Drop that knife," she ordered.

Fletcher's partner jerked his head up to look at her. "My Gawd! I think she means it, Jack," he said.

There was a long stillness, then Fletcher slowly unclenched his fingers and the knife clattered to the floor.

Elizabeth moved the rifle a fraction. "Now the bottle," she said.

The big man let it drop. No one moved.

Elizabeth, the rifle still levelled, said, "There is a gentleman with a blue kerchief around his neck, standing near the door. Go for the police, please, sir. This argument can be settled by the law. No one else will move."

"Wait!" Fletcher's partner said uneasily. "Look, lady, it weren't nothin' – just a little argument. There's no call to get police into it. We got the gold back. Me and Jack – well, we had too much, I guess. Eh, Jack?"

Jack nodded. "Yeah. I wouldn't have – Yeah."

The man with the blue kerchief looked enquiringly at Elizabeth.

"Very well," she said after a moment. She didn't lower the rifle.

"You," she said to the gold-thief, "had better go. Leave town. And if I were you, I'd do it now, and I wouldn't come back."

The man went quickly to the door and out.

"And, Mr Fletcher," Elizabeth added, "it would be most unfortunate for you and your partner if any misfortune befell that gentleman, as I'm sure you understand. Now I suggest you go your ways, and don't drink quite so much in the future. People dislike theft. They dislike murder even more. And," she added sharply as Fletcher stooped to pick up his knife, "I'd leave that where it is, if I were you."

He straightened up empty-handed, and he and his partner went out.

Elizabeth lowered the rifle and Maggie came quickly forward, picked up the knife and called into the awkward silence:

"Well, then, don't just stand there – I'll never make me fortune that way. What'll it be, then?"

There was general laughter and a rumble of conversation resumed as the men moved back toward the bar.

Maggie Doyle looked up at Elizabeth and a smile passed between them that only they really understood.

Elizabeth moved quietly back away from the head of the stairs, glad that no one could see how her hands, ice-steady when she had levelled the rifle at the murderous scene in the saloon, had begun to shake uncontrollably.

She glanced back as the saloon door was flung violently open and two policemen, pistols in hand, burst in. Instantly she put the rifle on the floor, out of sight from the room below.

Again silence fell as everyone turned to look at the troopers.

One, a bearded sergeant, demanded, "What's going on here?"

Maggie Doyle, in the act of pouring rum, looked at him in a fine imitation of astonishment. "I might ask you that very question, Sergeant."

"Someone fired a shot on these premises or close by, not five minutes ago."

"Really?" Maggie said eagerly. "Who?"

"That is precisely what we were wondering," the sergeant said drily. "Come, now, what's going on here? A shot was fired. You mean to tell me no one heard it?"

Dr Miller put his empty glass carefully on the bar. "We're not deaf, Sergeant. Yes, certainly I heard a noise, but it sounded to me like blasting in one of the mines."

There was a general murmur of agreement.

The sergeant looked at the floor where whisky and glass fragments were still spread. At the sound of the door opening Dr Miller had stepped casually on to the spot where the bullet had ploughed into the floor.

"How did that bottle come to be broken?" the sergeant demanded.

"Bottles usually break when you drop 'em, Sergeant," Maggie told him.

The policeman looked up at Elizabeth and automatically touched his cap.

"Perhaps you could tell me, madam: was a shot fired close by a few minutes ago?"

"Well, Sergeant," Elizabeth said doubtfully, "my little girl is ill in bed and I've been sitting with her – indeed, I was just coming downstairs to ask Mrs Doyle for some warm water from the kitchen. I'm a newcomer to the gold field and there are many sounds strange to me. But I should think I'd have heard a shot if it had been close by, wouldn't I?"

He eyed her thoughtfully for a moment. "I would have thought so, madam." He looked suspiciously around the saloon again and shrugged. "Come, Higgs," he said briefly to his constable, and they went.

Three

The spell of fine weather lasted just enough days to allow Robert and Bert Peters to finish the two-roomed cabin that was to be the Waldens' home.

As Dr Miller had predicted, Sarah suffered no more than bruises from her accident, and Elizabeth took the children each day and went to the hut to work at the building.

Sawn timber from the mill was in heavy demand and the Waldens had neither the time to wait for it nor the money to pay for it.

"But Bert knows how to build a snug little place from bark and slabs," Robert told Elizabeth.

"Snug," Elizabeth repeated, her face damp in the summer heat.

Robert grinned. "Weatherproof, then. Slab walls of roughly-split timber – that dray-driver was right about my hands, but they'll be toughened nicely for sinking my shaft. A bark roof – there are ways of laying bark to make it as water-tight as shingle any day. And you plaster the walls with mud and it sets beautifully. It's rather like wattle-and-daub, really."

"It really does work, Mrs Walden," Bert Peters assured her.

"What do you use for a floor?" Elizabeth asked.

"Beaten earth. You just thump and pound the ground hard and level."

Robert laughed at her look and put his arms around her. "Oh, my Elizabeth," he said against her hair. "One day you shall have the finest mansion in the country, and servants and carriages and all the rest of it. But this is the adventure – earning all those things."

He held her away a little so that he could look down at her. "When we look back on this and laugh about the little hardships we had, we'll think these were the best days of all."

Looking at the love of life that danced in his brown eyes, she could almost believe they were.

And so she learned to plaster walls with mud, and level a floor and pound it hard. And when her back ached too much and her hands were too sore, she got out books and taught the children their lessons.

Bert Peters built a fireplace and chimney from stone, skilled hands laying loose stones quickly and efficiently, so that Elizabeth would be able to cook over an open hearth until such time as they may be able to install a wood-burning iron stove.

Watching Bert work, Elizabeth said, "You're a skilled stonemason, Mr Peters. Why didn't you go on following the trade?"

"Instead of following the gold?" He smiled. "I had no job when news of this strike came through. I'd followed the gold all around Victoria and always finished up taking labourer's work to feed myself, so what did I have to lose? I like to move, meet new people, see what's happening in the world. Chasing gold gives men like me a good excuse for drifting, Mrs Walden. Makes it respectable, like. But the truth is, there are some of us just enjoy wandering. I never had no money. I've never really wanted none. Lord knows what I'd do with it if I suddenly found I had some."

He grinned, teeth flashing in his black beard. "I must admit I'd be quite happy to be rich. But I'm also quite happy to be poor. Living's the thing that matters — not money; and I enjoy living."

The windows of the shack were wooden shutters hinged at the top with leather and propped open with a piece of timber. The door also hung on leather hinges. The division of the hut into two rooms was achieved by hanging a piece of hessian across it.

Robert and Bert carried in the Waldens' trunk and valises and the few bits of furniture they had brought on the boat and persuaded the dray-driver to carry on the laborious journey from Maryborough.

"Well, Mrs Walden," Robert said, surveying the hut, "St James Palace it's not, but it's our first step on the way to our mansion. I feel I should at least carry you over the threshold."

She looked at him and smiled. "If anyone happened to be watching they'd think you were mad."

"Then dammit, I will." He scooped her up easily in his arms and carried her inside while the children applauded delightedly.

He set her down and, laughing, she looked up at him. "Now I have to go shopping."

He let her go and a little frown creased between his eyes. "Shopping?"

"But of course!" She gestured at the nearly-empty hut. "We need all manner of things before I can even cook a meal — a couple of cook-pots, a tin dish to wash up in — and wash ourselves and our clothes in — even a table, if one can buy such a thing here. And, not least important, we have to have food."

"I can make a table easily enough. It mightn't be a

Sheraton, but it'd serve for eating off."

"Fine. I imagine Trent's General Store will have just about everything else we need."

"Yes, I imagine so." He moved restlessly and Elizabeth stood suddenly very still.

"Robert? What's wrong?" Her voice was quiet and unaccusing, but in the chill inside her she knew the answer before she asked the question.

"Well –" He fiddled a moment with a window-catch.

"We do need more than a table," she reminded.

"Yes, yes, of course!" He swung around to face her. "Stupid of me, I know, but I just didn't think about the fact we'd need things so soon. I thought –"

"That there'd be a chance to win it back?"

He nodded miserably.

"There never is, Robert."

He smacked one fist into the other palm. "But I was on a winning streak! It looked as if I couldn't lose!"

Her voice low, her face expressionless, she said, "How much have we left?"

Robert shook his head.

After a moment Elizabeth said very quietly, "What are we to do?"

"We'll just have to ask John Trent for credit. He seems a decent sort of fellow. Well," he said defensively, "it's only for a little while – until I can get the shaft down."

"I see," Elizabeth said.

"Oh, come on!" he urged. "There's gold all around us – I can't be *that* unlucky!"

"A winning streak," she murmured.

"Look, sweetheart, I'm sorry," he said. "Truly I am. I didn't mean –"

"It's all right," she cut him short, almost soothingly. "It's done, there's no point in fussing about it. Let's just hope Mr Trent will listen to you."

"Well —" Robert rubbed his chin. "I think it might be better if *you* went to him. No," he caught her hands as she took a breath to protest, "I'm not just ducking out. But John Trent has the reputation of being a gentleman, though not kindly disposed to gamblers. He'd listen to you — how could any man not? And he'd probably throw me out on my unworthy ear. It's true, Elizabeth."

He stood looking down at her earnestly.

Finally she sighed. "Very well, Robert. I'll go."

He kissed the top of her head. "That's my Elizabeth. I'll never know why you married me, but I'm awfully glad you did."

She turned away quickly at the prick of tears behind her eyes and said lightly, "Well, you'd better at least start digging. That's the only collateral I have to offer Mr Trent, unless he's prepared to accept my word that my allowance from my father is due soon — depending on the sailings from England."

Robert grinned and picked up his hat. "I'll have that shaft down before Trent stops being dazzled by my lovely wife. And I'll bet you we're sitting right over a seam of solid gold."

When he went out, Edward looked gravely at his mother. "What happened to our money, Mother?"

"Your father was looking after it and he lost it, that's all."

"Father often loses money, doesn't he?" Edward asked shrewdly. "How does he lose it?"

"Well, he's a little careless, I'm afraid."

"Maybe someone stole it," Sarah put in hopefully. "Mr Peters told me some bad men sometimes steal other men's gold that they've dug up. Will Daddy dig up some gold?"

"I'd like to see a hold-up," Edward said, brandishing an imaginary pistol and shouting, "Bang! Bang!" with great gusto.

As Robert was working close to the hut, Elizabeth left the children to their game and, putting on her hat more as protection from the harsh sun than as a concession to either fashion or the proprieties which looked askance at a woman going down the street hatless, set out to walk into the town. It was a little distance, as Robert had been forced to choose his spot, not in the richest area, but in what he judged to be the most promising place among the remaining land.

As she walked away from his store, John Trent stood in the doorway, watching her.

Dr Miller, who had gone into the store for tobacco, looked at him with twinkling eyes.

"Well, John! A busy man like you, offering to deliver goods when the lady has a perfectly fit husband who could collect them?"

"If her husband showed up on my doorstep at the moment I'd punch his teeth in, that's the reason," the big blond man said shortly. "She'd rather die than say a word against him, I reckon, but I know why they haven't any money, and so do you."

"Well, now," Abraham Miller said cheerfully, "every man's entitled to one weakness, surely. There are worse ones than gambling, young John, and don't you forget it."

"It's not only that," John Trent said. "He hasn't the guts to come to me himself and admit he's broke to the world, has he? Oh, no, because that's a state that doesn't befit a gentleman. So he sends his wife. It doesn't matter that she finds it even more humiliating, does it? Not that she'd let it show. Oh, no. All the poise of a duchess going to a ball."

"Hmm." Dr Miller took a long pull at his pipe. "And if Captain Walden had come to you himself and asked for credit, would you have given it him?"

"No way! I've precious little patience with gambling, and a lot less faith it'll pay off."

Dr Miller chuckled wickedly. "There you are, then. Walden isn't necessarily unfeeling toward his wife: he's just practical. Anyway, you should get to know Robert Walden. He's no villain, young John; he's a very nice fellow. Think I'll invite you and the Waldens around to my house some evening."

John eyed him suspiciously.

Dr Miller shook his head. "I'm not drunk and I'm not up to mischief. Matter of fact, John, I fully share your admiration for Mrs Walden, and I'd like her to meet some people – make friends. Very lonely for a woman like her in a mining town. The Burtons are due in town for a couple of days before too long: I've a feeling Molly Burton and Mrs Walden would get on just fine. Mind you, Mrs Walden and Maggie Doyle seem to have become good friends."

"Maggie Doyle!" John Trent stared at him in astonishment. "I can't imagine what Mrs Walden would find in common with a rough-tongued woman like Maggie Doyle."

The doctor took his pipe from his mouth and looked at John, bright eyes quizzical behind his gold-rimmed glasses.

"John Trent," he said solemnly, "you do have a lot to learn, don't you?"

He pulled out a heavy gold watch and looked at it thoughtfully.

"It is two in the afternoon and I am perfectly sober. This grave condition must be arrested. Remember, I shall be inviting you when the Burtons come, and you see you accept."

And he went down the steps with the curiously springy stride that was characteristic of him, leaving John Trent smiling and shaking his head.

Four

Dr Miller was right on two counts: John Trent had to admit a degree of liking for the devil-may-care gaiety of Robert Walden; and Elizabeth and Molly Burton struck up an immediate friendship.

Molly was thirty, red-headed and as vivacious as her husband – who was perhaps ten years older – was quiet and reserved. The Burtons had a large and well-established farming and grazing property, a few miles out of the town, selected and settled long before the gold was found.

"We never imagined we'd have a whole town suddenly spring to life right beside us," Molly laughed. "Why don't you bring the children and come out to spend a few days while your husband is busy burrowing down to his fortune? We've a nice house and it's pretty, there. We're on a hill looking down to the river and we've planted trees – even willows, would you believe, just like home – and I've a bit of a garden. I do love flowers. Could you come? You will let her come, Captain Walden, won't you?"

Robert laughed. "If I can make two beautiful women happy at once, how could I refuse? If Elizabeth and the children can travel to the farm with you, and anyone can tell me where I can beg or borrow or if necessary steal a horse and buggy to bring them home again, of course they may go."

"I can arrange the horse and buggy," Dr Miller said.

So Elizabeth and the children went to Oak Bend, the Burtons' highly prosperous property, named for the needle-leafed casuarinas, commonly called sheoaks, which clustered the river banks.

Early April had taken much of the sweltering heat out of summer and the rains had lessened with the onset of autumn. Elizabeth was enchanted by the farm, and the children were riotously delighted with space around them and animals to watch.

Jim Burton grew pumpkins and corn and potatoes, and fat cattle grazed his extensive property. The six-roomed house with its wide verandahs, high ceilings and scrubbed floor-boards scattered with rugs of hide and a couple of dingo-pelts, seemed to Elizabeth a palace after the Waldens' shack.

"But most of all," she told Molly one day, "I envy you the – the *security*, the solidness, the knowledge that this is your home and here you'll stay. There's a permanence – I never realized how much I needed it till suddenly I didn't have it any more."

Molly Burton looked out of the window to where the children were playing at driving a buggy with no horse, and her green eyes softened in a slow smile.

"And I would give it all away for two children like yours."

There was a little silence, and then Elizabeth said, "How stupid I am! You're right, of course. Here I am with so much, and still feeling sorry for myself. No, not really. Because of course I wouldn't exchange Robert and the children for –"

She stopped, suddenly aware that Molly's gaze had gone beyond the children and that she had stiffened in uneasiness.

"What is it?" Elizabeth demanded, stepping toward the window.

"Call the children inside," Molly said, her voice quick and low. "And bolt the doors and latch the windows."

Elizabeth saw a party of naked dark men walking up from near the river.

"Aborigines! But surely there's no danger from them? They're friendly, aren't they?"

"Call the children!" Molly ordered sharply, hurrying to close the windows.

Elizabeth obeyed and, as the children came in, shut and bolted the door.

"What's wrong, Mother?" Edward wanted to know.

"I don't know. Aunt Molly wants us to close up the house."

She turned questioningly as Molly came back. Molly shrugged.

"Maybe I'm just nervous. But Jim is away out in the paddocks and there are no men around. It's only that these natives are strangers I've never seen before – they're not the locals at all. And there are only men, and they're painted and carrying spears. Maybe a hunting party. Equally maybe a war party seeking revenge for something or other. And aborigines don't always have reason to feel kindly to Europeans. I don't expect they mean any harm, but I just don't know. They'll probably just walk straight by and go on their way."

They didn't.

They came directly to the house – twenty armed men, their faces and bodies daubed with ochre – and stood for a while talking and gesturing among themselves. While the women watched from behind curtains and the children stood wide-eyed and silent against the wall, the dark men examined the buggy with much exclaiming, and then turned towards the house and called several times.

Elizabeth asked softly, "What are they saying?"

Molly shook her head. "I don't know. They don't belong to our local tribe. It's a different dialect. I can't pick a single word. Closing up the house obviously didn't convince them there's no one here. I expect they can see smoke rising from the chimney."

The party moved closer to the house and several men called again, more loudly, demandingly.

Molly looked at Elizabeth. "Can you use a shotgun?" she murmured.

Elizabeth nodded, her eyes darkening with horror. "But –"

Molly slipped silently away and was back in moments with the gun and a box of cartridges.

"We'll hide the children," she whispered. "Come."

Elizabeth and the children followed wordlessly. The women's fear had reached Edward and Sarah, and Edward held his sister's hand firmly, and both were instinctively quiet.

In the bedroom Elizabeth and the children were using, one corner was turned into a closet by a curtain hung across it. Molly motioned the children behind the curtain.

Elizabeth kissed Sarah and smiled. "Now, we think it's just a game, sweetheart. But be a good girl and do what Edward says."

She looked at her son. Eight years seemed very little experience of life to enable him to cope with something like this.

"Edward, those men may be friends, or they may mean to kill us. We don't know because we can't understand what they're saying. If they mean to hurt us you'll hear shooting. But stay where you are unless the men come into the house or set it on fire. Stay still and quiet till then. Understand?"

Edward nodded.

"If they get in or set the house on fire, get out of the window and run as hard as you both can for –" She stopped and looked at Molly.

"That patch of trees behind the hayshed," Molly supplied. "Hide there till Uncle Jim or some other white man comes."

Elizabeth let the curtain drop back into place and the women went quickly back to the front window. "A thousand to one it'll never come to that," Molly declared. "But if it should, they'll be out of sight of the natives if they go that way."

Elizabeth knew it was by no means so sure, but she said nothing as Molly picked up the shotgun, loaded it and handed it to her.

"Cover me," Molly ordered. "I'm going out to talk to them."

"No!" Elizabeth said sharply. "You mustn't."

Molly shrugged. The men's shouts had become louder, more aggressive.

"If they mean to murder us, we can't stop them, with one shotgun against twenty armed warriors. I may as well give friendliness a try. Jim has a very good relationship with the aborigines. Word of his good reputation may have got around, and this is a friendly visit. We could turn it sour by not showing ourselves."

"Then let me go out." Elizabeth smiled. "You're probably a much better shot."

Molly shook her head and unbolted the door. "I know a few words of the local tribe's dialect. These men might understand a little of it. Bolt this behind me."

She went out and shut the door. Feeling like a traitor, Elizabeth obeyed and slid the bolt home. She knew why Molly had ordered it: if the aborigines meant murder, Molly would not live to get back into the house anyway, and Elizabeth might as well fight for as long as she could, to give the children a better survival chance against fewer attackers.

The instant Molly appeared the natives fell silent. For a moment she stood still, and so did the dark men. Then she walked toward them, speaking what Elizabeth guessed were words of greeting.

One older man drove his spear into the ground and stepped forward from the group with a few gutteral words.

Elizabeth shifted the shotgun a couple of degrees to aim it at one young man who seemed the most restless of the group.

Molly seemed unable to understand what the older man was saying. Elizabeth caught one word, repeated a number of times.

Smiling and nodding, Molly turned to come back to the house and Elizabeth's finger tightened a little on the trigger.

No one moved to stop Molly, and Elizabeth stepped quickly to the door and unbolted it. Molly came in, shut the door and leaned against it, eyes closed in a white face.

"What is it?" Elizabeth demanded.

Molly opened her eyes and smiled ruefully. "Just a bad case of blue funk. I'm all right. But I don't know what they want. I *think* it's food, and I *think* they don't mean harm — at least as long as they get whatever it is they want. Let's have a look in the pantry."

She took some flour and sugar in calico bags, and a batch of biscuits she had baked the previous day, and carried them out while Elizabeth took up her position at the window again.

The aborigines gathered around Molly, all but the older man still holding their spears, while Elizabeth watched them along the barrel of the gun, tensed for the slightest sign of aggression, thinking bitterly that it was far more difficult to give her friend any kind of cover now that she was clustered about by dark bodies.

Fingers were thrust exploringly into the flour and sugar and licked thoughtfully, with some appreciation of the sugar. Molly bit a piece off one of the biscuits and ate it, then handed the remainder to the senior man. The biscuits were eaten with relish, handed around among the men, and Elizabeth could sense that Molly was relaxing, still trying to talk to the men in the local dialect. Eventually, when Elizabeth felt she was aching all over with the tension, Molly smiled, waved in gesture of farewell, and began to walk back to the house.

At once the old man snapped out a sharp word and Molly turned. He held out his hand and repeated the word they had used before.

Molly shook her head and spread her hands helplessly, trying to explain that she didn't understand.

The whole group took up the demand: one word repeated over and over, impatiently, taking on increasing menace. Molly nodded and came quickly to the door as Elizabeth drew the bolt.

"What do they want?" Elizabeth asked urgently.

Molly shook her head. "I wish under Heaven I knew. They think I'm just refusing it, I'm afraid, and they're growing impatient. I've a feeling one or two of them might be quite prepared to come and take it, whatever it is."

She shivered. "Yet I think if I could give it to them they'd go away content."

"I wonder –" Elizabeth hesitated. "I wonder if it's salt? I've heard somewhere that sometimes the aborigines whose territory is away from the sea sometimes develop a craving for salt."

Molly ran into the pantry. "You could well be right.

Why didn't I think of that? There" – tipping a generous quantity into a calico bag – "if that's what they want, that should keep them happy."

She took a deep breath and Elizabeth nodded and picked up the gun again as Molly went out.

The men were standing silent, frowning and restless. Molly went unhesitatingly up to the old man and held out the calico bag, smiling. Elizabeth thought she would never see anything more courageous.

The old man dipped his finger in the salt and licked it, and in an instant his manner changed as his face crinkled in a smile. The others gathered around, tasting also, with much nodding.

Then they gathered up their weapons and their bags of flour and sugar and with a few brief gestures of salute, filed past the house and away.

Very slowly Elizabeth lowered the gun, broke the breech and removed the cartridge. Very slowly Molly walked back to the house.

They smiled at each other and Molly Burton said, "Sure, it's a lovely woman you are, Mrs Walden."

"I rather felt," Elizabeth told her, "you weren't too bad, yourself. Let's go and get the children. They weren't too bad, either."

"I've a feeling," Molly said gravely, "this country may produce some good strains of human beings."

To Elizabeth's surprise it was not Robert, but Bert Peters who drove out to Oak Ridge to take her and the children back to town in Dr Miller's buggy.

"Now, there's nothing wrong with Robert, Mrs Walden," Bert assured her. "He asked me to come – paid me, if it'll make you feel better – because he said he was working on a surprise for you. And don't ask me what it is," he added with a laugh. "I'm sworn to secrecy."

Elizabeth smiled. "I wouldn't spoil his fun, anyway. But I do just wonder," she added to Molly Burton, "if he's somehow managed to get a piece or two of decent furniture."

For some reason Bert seemed to think that hilarious, and Elizabeth and the children spent much of the time on the jolting drive back to town playing games at guessing what Robert had in store for them.

It was late afternoon and the lengthening shadows of autumn pointed dark fingers eastwards when they drove into town.

"There are a lot of people around our claim!" Edward said as they came in sight of it. "There was hardly anybody near us before, because I heard a man say Father would never find gold down there. What are they all doing, Mr Peters?"

Elizabeth clutched Bert's arm. "The flag! Bert, the red flag is on Robert's claim!"

Bert nodded, laughing. "The flag every miner must hoist when he strikes gold, or forfeit his claim. That's right, Mrs Walden. Robert's bottomed on gold."

Five

He clambered up from the shaft grimy and sweat-soaked and haggard with exhaustion, but his brown eyes danced exultation as he flung his arms around Elizabeth.

"We've won, my Elizabeth, we've won!"

After a long moment he took his lips from hers and laughed down at her. "I'll swear you've never been kissed by such a dirty man!"

She laughed back at him. "Nor liked it more."

"Father, can I come down the shaft?" Edward demanded. "I can help you dig."

Robert knelt and put one arm around each of his children in a welcoming hug.

"I'm sure you could help me. But if you came down with me, your mother and Sarah wouldn't have a man to look after them and I couldn't be happy about leaving them then, could I?"

Edward nodded importantly. "I see. All right. But Father, can I see the gold?"

"Me, too!" cried Sarah, jigging about. "I want to see the gold!"

"All right." Robert grinned. "Come into the house."

They went in, Bert Peters with them, and Robert took a chamois bag which he had tied around his waist.

"Robert!" Elizabeth cried in alarm. "You don't carry it all with you?"

"No, no. I've given some to John Trent to pay him what we owed, and I sold some to pay the other debts we had, and to have a little ready cash."

He opened the bag and spilled half a dozen small rough nuggets on the pine table.

Elizabeth touched them wonderingly. "It doesn't look like something to drive people to crazy lengths to get it, does it?"

The children exclaimed over the rough pieces, and suddenly Elizabeth became aware that Bert Peters, standing very still, had said nothing. She glanced up. He was looking oddly at Robert.

"Is this all?" he asked quietly. "Haven't you found any more since yesterday?"

"No," Robert said. "Not yet. I must have just driven off the seam. I thought it would run west, but it looks as if it doesn't. I'll have to drive the other way, or just work around until I hit the seam again."

"What about the others – the new ones who've just started their shafts?"

Robert laughed. "Give them a chance, man! They haven't bottomed yet."

When the men on the surrounding claims did bottom their shafts, they found no gold.

And Robert, though he worked like a fiend, found no more. It had been an isolated pocket, and nothing more than that.

"It doesn't look good," he said finally as he sat wearily at the scrubbed table one evening after many days of frenzied toil. It was as near to an admission of defeat as Elizabeth had ever heard from him.

Dr Miller and Bert Peters had come in with the darkness to ask how he was faring.

"It's the luck of the game," Bert said sympathetically.

"At least," Abraham Miller said, "you found *some* gold. There's still a chance there's more. Now in our mine – Bert's and mine – we've unearthed – or I should say Bert's unearthed – what's the tally now, Bert? Several hundred tons of dirt and rock, four scorpions and one black snake, isn't it? But nary a speck of the yellow stuff."

Elizabeth looked at Dr Miller. "No one's finding gold in the little mines any longer, are they? It's only the big ones, with machinery and great teams of men that are succeeding. The alluvial is almost all gone. The day of the little miner is over, isn't it?"

Miller hesitated. "One can't ever be sure. As Bert says, it's all in the luck of the game. But it does seem there are precious few fortunes left for the individual pick and shovel."

"Robert," Elizabeth said gently, "why not give it up? Take a job in one of the big mines if you must mine, though the idea of you working down in those great pits terrifies me."

He laughed. "It needn't. I'm not going swinging a pick for any big company."

"Then let's go into business, like John Trent, or take up land like the Burtons, even though it would have to be in a very small way."

He looked at her. "You'd really like that, wouldn't you? You'd like a nice, quiet, settled life. Well, my Elizabeth, you shall have it as soon as I make enough money, I promise you. But it needs capital to set up a business or start a farm on a worthwhile scale, and I just don't have that capital. So I'll have to go on looking for gold."

She turned away to tend the fire and, watching her,

Robert said, "I'm not really all that crazy, Elizabeth. Lots of shafts have been abandoned because they drew a blank, and then other people have come and reopened them and struck the gold. Why, the great Curtis nugget on this field was found in a shaft that was thought to be empty."

He grinned. "Why, even Bert still pokes around that mine he and the doctor have. That's what makes a man chase the gold in the first place: it doesn't matter how many people tell you you're daft, you just *know* you're going to strike it rich."

Dr Miller looked at Bert with a twinkle. "*Do* you still poke around our mine, Bert?"

Bert shrugged. "Sure. It's just the way Robert says, I guess. You can't really stop. You go to bed at night fed up with the thing. You know it's a shicer and you've just wasted your time and your muscles are sore for the last time from working down that useless rotten hole. Then you start to think: maybe if you'd swung your pick just once more – And so you can hardly wait to get down there again next morning."

He nodded. "Oh, yes, I still go down and chip around sometimes when I haven't anything else to do."

He looked at Dr Miller. "I wish you'd let me buy out your share of the rotten thing, Doc. You stood by me when I hadn't a bean to buy a shovel with, but now I've taken a few jobs around the town I can pay you back. It was my idea to stake the claim there. No occasion for you to lose money over my bad judgment."

Miller laughed. "Rubbish, boy, rubbish! You're always worrying about it, wanting to buy my share. But I wouldn't sell my share in that shaft for anything. I mean to say, what's the sense in being on a gold-field if you don't try your hand at mining, eh? And I'm too fat and lazy to swing a pick, so while you do the work it all suits me very well.

Anyway, I like a bit of a gamble now and then."

He stood up. "Speaking of gambles, I expect there'll be a spot of gold won and lost without any digging on race day. Come down to Maggie's place, Bert, and I'll buy you a drink."

Though Robert laboured doggedly, driving a lateral tunnel in his search for the reef whose edge he still believed he must have just brushed, his questing pick turned up no gleam of yellow. It was slow work, wearying and tedious, especially for a man working alone. The tunnel roof and walls had to be shored with timber every bit of the way to guard against the dreaded rock-fall that could entomb a miner under tons of rock and earth in a couple of seconds. The same shoring had had to be done on the vertical walls of the shaft, but it was neither so slow nor so dangerous. The earth and rock had to be filled into buckets and then windlassed to the surface.

Robert's optimism remained, even though the weeks ran on. As the much-discussed race-day drew close he became gaily confident that whatever the mine did about denying him riches, he could win on the race-track.

"Even I," Elizabeth confided to Maggie Doyle, "have some small hope he might win. He does know horses very well."

"Horses or gold or cards," Maggie said drily. "The chances of a fortune are about the same."

Elizabeth smiled. "I hardly think he'll win a fortune at the races. He won't have enough money to start with! But I would like to see him win a little."

She looked momentarily wistful. "Everyone needs to win sometimes."

"Meaning you don't think he'll ever win with the gold?"

"How can he? The gold is gone, for the small miner.

People are slowly learning that, and leaving the field."

She glanced quickly at Maggie. "Will it affect you? Will you have to go if too many people leave?"

Maggie shook her head. "I haven't noticed a great decline in the general thirst. No, my dear, this town isn't like some gold-rush towns, a great boom and then the bubble bursts. This town will go on because the farmlands and the timber will keep it alive – not quite so hectic as at its peak, but it will last. And the gold's not finished by a long way, not for the big mines."

She smiled. "If you think Gympie's dying, wait till race day!"

It seemed everyone in town was talking about the picnic races.

It was the one day of the year when the whole town, and many of the farmers and timbergetters in the surrounding countryside, took a holiday. The crude track was set out on flat ground a little way out of town and anyone who owned a horse could enter it in a race.

Most people took picnic lunches and water for making tea was boiled over open fires. Some enterprising vendors set up stalls which sold food, and liquor booths did a roaring trade. It gave people a rare opportunity to meet old friends and make new acquaintances, and the races themselves provided suspense and excitement, and bookmakers did a lively business as miners rich with new gold saw a chance to double it, and miners down on their luck saw a chance that the horses might win them some of the gold their picks had failed to find.

The day was glorious: crisp and clear as a Queensland end-of-winter day can be – a day filled with sunshine and optimism.

Robert looked over the horses carefully with skilled eyes.

Dr Miller came along and watched his examination of the race entrants with a smile.

"Well, young Robert, a cavalryman should know horseflesh better than I do. What about a tip for an old man?"

Robert grinned. "Brown King in the first race."

Abraham Miller looked at Elizabeth. "Is he to be relied on, Mrs Walden?"

"I couldn't guarantee anything, Doctor," Elizabeth smiled. "But he is a good judge of horses."

"My father knows more about horses than anyone else here, Dr Miller, I'll bet," Edward said earnestly.

Dr Miller looked down at him and ruffled his fair hair affectionately. "That's good enough for me, son. Brown King it is." He glanced at Robert. "That's a fine son you have there, young Robert."

"The best there is," Robert agreed. "And I have a very beautiful young lady for a daughter, too."

Sarah, uninterested in the compliments, said, "Can I have a pony one day, Daddy?"

"You certainly shall."

"As nice as Brown King?"

"Even nicer."

"And can I ride him in the races?" Her brown eyes were sparkling.

"Mmm. Well, we'll have to see about that."

The men went off to place their bets, Edward striding confidently along beside his father while Elizabeth watched them with a little smile.

Brown King in fact came in eighth in a field of twelve.

Dr Miller looked at Robert in mock disgust. "And what's your tip for the second race, so I'll know not to waste my hard-earned money on it?"

Robert laughed. "Backing out after one loss? Come, Doctor, where's your sense of adventure? I'm backing Trident."

"Poor horse doesn't know it, but he doesn't have a chance, then," Miller said gloomily.

Trident won.

"Bah!" Dr Miller grunted. "My gambling career is ended. I need some refreshment, so I'll bid you good day. Not that I don't find the company charming, Mrs Walden," he added, lifting his hat. "But if I stand around watching your husband bet I shall end the day either penniless or a nervous wreck."

And he marched off toward the nearest liquor booth.

The horse Robert backed won the third race. He increased the amout he bet and won again on the fourth.

There was a long break then between races while people settled down to their picnic lunches, sitting on rugs spread on the grass in the shade of the eucalypts beside the track – not because the day was hot, but because the ladies were anxious to defend their skins against the sun, using shade as well as the protection afforded by their long-sleeved frocks, scarves and large hats.

Robert was restless and ate very little and talked too much, like a man who has had a little too much to drink.

Elizabeth watched him in growing uneasiness. This was Robert at his most reckless – Robert on a winning streak. She thought thankfully of the money she had hidden away, as she had done many times. It was little enough, but it was some protection. This man who would deny his family nothing would risk every penny they owned on the turn of a card or the beat of a hoof.

He took out his winnings and counted the money carefully.

"Let me hold some while you go and put your bet on the

next race," Elizabeth suggested, carefully casual. "There could be pick-pockets around today."

He pushed the money back into his pocket just as casually. "No, it's all right," he said, and got up and sauntered off to the bookmaker's stand.

When he came back she asked, "Which one have you picked?"

"Ringer. He's a big grey." He was quiet now, not wanting to talk, tense and anxious for the start of the race. Elizabeth knew why he was so restless and she felt the palms of her hands sticky with perspiration.

As the horses thundered toward the winning-post and the judges, the big grey ranged up on the outside and came in the winner by three lengths.

Robert let out a whoop of joy and flung his arms around Elizabeth. "We've done it, we've done it! I put every bit of the money on him and he came home!"

When he came back from the bookmaker he pulled out the money and showed it to Elizabeth and the children. "Just over two hundred pounds!" he exulted. "Let's go and have another look at the horses for the Cup."

The next race, the Miner's Cup, was the main race of the day, carrying the biggest prize-money and naturally attracting the best horses in the district. Favourite was a fine black stallion whose coat gleamed in the sun as it flexed over rippling muscles.

Robert looked him over very carefully, then spent some time studying a bay gelding; but finally he went to a chestnut mare, stood looking at her for a while, and ran his hand along her shoulder and down to her fetlock, watched by a wary owner.

Robert straightened up. "She'll win," he said.

The owner grinned. "I hope you're right, mister. There's some tough opposition."

"That's true. But over that distance, with the light weight she's carrying, she'll win. I'm sure of it."

He started toward the bookmaker's stand and Elizabeth caught his arm.

"Robert, don't."

"Don't bet?" he raised a quizzical eyebrow.

"You know what I mean. Please don't put all the money on this race. What you've won is wonderful. Let's just be glad, and keep it."

He laughed, his eyes fever-bright. "Stop now, when I'm on a winning streak?"

"Winning streaks always end."

"This one isn't ended. I'm sure of it."

"Put some of the money on, then. But not all of it. Please."

He shook his head. "Listen, my Elizabeth. This mare is racing at ten to one. She can turn two hundred pounds into two thousand. Think of it! That's a fortune! Enough to buy the best land in the country – a farm like Jim and Molly Burton have and better. And a house to dream of. And that's what I mean to win for you, and nothing is going to stop me."

She let him go. To have done anything else would have created a scene, and nothing she could say would stop Robert when he was in this frame of mind.

And she had to admit that his mood of elation was contagious. She took his arm as the horses lined up at the start, and he looked down at her, his eyes gay, and put his other hand over hers.

A stilled expectancy tensed the crowd and everyone turned toward the track. Men and boys clambered into trees for the best vantage points, and Edward and two other boys about his age climbed on one of the lower limbs of a eucalypt just behind where Robert and Elizabeth were standing.

"My father might win a lot of money on this race," Edward told the other boys, his eyes sparkling.

Sarah clutched her mother's hand and craned her neck eagerly to watch the horses, not quite understanding what it was all about, but infected with the excitement.

The horses were to make three circuits of the track, and on the far side it was difficult to see which horse was in front, but the field was well spread out as jockeys held their mounts slightly in check, saving their energy and waiting for a chance to manoeuvre for a good run to the post.

As they came around the track the last time the black stallion was well out in front and the crowd began to cheer their favourite, urging him on. But now the other riders began to put pressure on their horses, and the gap began to close, though it seemed no one could catch the black.

Elizabeth felt tight and cold inside.

With a hundred and twenty yards to go, the mare Robert had backed somehow came up beside the favourite and hit the front. Even above the roar of the crowd Elizabeth heard Robert's shout of triumph.

And in the same instant there was a cracking sound as the branch on which Edward and his companions had climbed snapped under their excited weight, spilling the three small boys on the ground.

Two of them jumped up at once, laughing, but Edward made a strangely groping attempt to get to his knees, and then sprawled face down on the grass. The laughter of the other two faltered and became a scream of horror that made everyone nearby whirl around to look.

Robert leapt forward to kneel beside his son, shouting: "Get Dr Miller! Try the liquor booth. Hurry!"

Even as he ran toward Edward he had been pulling off his coat, and as he knelt he jerked his tie loose. "Keep Sarah away!"

A woman in the crowd, white faced, quickly picked up

the little girl and carried her away.

Edward had fallen on a broken bottle whose razor-sharp edge had slashed his throat.

Robert tore off his shirt and folded it swiftly into a pad to press firmly against the wound to try to staunch the flow of blood. Edward did not move.

"Robert?" Elizabeth's voice, barely a whisper, reached him above the noise of the crowd which, except for the nearby few, knew nothing of the accident.

He raised his eyes from Edward to find Elizabeth kneeling on the other side of the little boy, holding tightly to his hand. Robert said simply, "I don't know."

Then he looked down at Edward again and shouted in anguish, "Where's that damned doctor?"

Someone said, "They've gone to fetch him." And there was an uneasy silence.

After what seemed an unbearable time a voice could be heard grumbling, "Dammit, don't push a man. Kids are always cutting themselves. Mothers get in a panic all the time. That's all it is. Mothers get in a panic."

Steadied by a man on either side, Dr Miller slowly wove his way through the crowd as shocked onlookers stepped back to make way.

"Well, well, what've we got, eh?" Miller said cheerfully as he came in sight of the Waldens. "Young Edward, eh? What's he been up to?"

He motioned Robert away and knelt beside the boy, moving the pad of Robert's shirt carefully, hands still steady in spite of his alcohol intake.

Robert went to Elizabeth and helped her to her feet and stood holding her.

After a couple of long minutes Dr Miller very slowly stood up.

"I'm sorry, Mrs Walden," he said. "He's dead."

Six

There was a stricken silence. Then Robert, soaked in his son's blood, let Elizabeth go and stepped toward Dr Miller.

"You let him die," he said. His voice was as quiet and as full of menace as a taipan poised to strike. "You dirty drunk, you let him die. I'll kill you for that."

Two or three men in the crowd, sensing Robert's grief-maddened fury, jumped forward and caught him by the arms.

"Let me go, damn you!" Robert snarled, fighting to break free. "He let my son die because he was too damned drunk to walk!"

Elizabeth, blind and deaf to everything around her, sank slowly to her knees beside Edward. Very carefully, as if not to disturb him, she took one of his hands in both hers, holding it as if she might keep the warmth of life in it.

She didn't cry, but all the unsheddable tears rose inside her in a terrible agony.

She wanted to shout that it was a lie – a foul and fearsome lie. Edward couldn't be dead. All that life – all that glowing exuberant life, ended before it had barely begun?

But the pain that dulled her senses told her it was no lie.

She did not move, even when Abraham Miller took off his coat and stooped to lay it gently over Edward.

Miller stood straight and looked at Robert.

"I know how you feel," he said quietly. "But I give you my word that, drunk or sober, if I'd been standing beside him when it happened, there was nothing I could do."

"There's something I can do," Robert said threshing and straining in the grip of the men who held him. "I can break your bloody neck!"

"Robert!" A big blond man thrust his way through the crowd. "For God's sake, man!" John Trent said. "Your wife! Your wife needs you."

Robert stood suddenly still and looked dazedly at John. "Yes," he said after a moment, as if he were waking from a nightmare. "Yes."

His captors released their grip and he began to walk toward the still-kneeling Elizabeth. Then he turned and looked back at Dr Miller. "But one day, Miller," he said slowly and clearly, "I'll kill you for this."

In the stricken days that followed Elizabeth was sharply conscious, even through her own anguish, of the strange black mood that gripped Robert.

No man could have been kinder or more thoughtful to her and Sarah. If he heard her stir in the night, wakeful with grief, he would at once move close to her and put his arms around her, gently and without passion, holding her as one might hold a child, trying to ease the ache of emptiness.

He took Sarah for walks, right away from the ugliness of the town and into the fringe of the bush, where he showed her the birds and the places where the little furred bandicoots had burrowed in the earth during the night in search of grubs or other edibles. He read to her from the children's books he and Elizabeth had brought with them.

He insisted that Elizabeth go with him and Sarah on their walks unless one of her friends among the women in the town was with her for company. He suggested that Elizabeth and Sarah go out to Oak Bend, the Burtons' farm, for a while.

Elizabeth said, "Will you come too?"

He shook his head. "Not yet."

"Then I shan't go, either."

And all the time he moved like a man sleepwalking. Even when he forced himself to talk, to make conversation, his voice was strangely flat, as if talking were something which required almost more effort than he could give.

He ate little and slept little. Several times Elizabeth woke to find him sitting at the rough table in the dark, a whisky bottle in his hand, though he was not drunk. Nor was he drunk once in those ten days when he moved in shock. Somehow Elizabeth thought she would have been less afraid if he had been drunk.

Although he talked with her with complete courtesy if she started a conversation, she felt she could not reach him. It was as if a part of his mind were somewhere else, busy with its own thoughts.

Elizabeth could never remember, afterwards, who had told them, or at what point they had learned, that the mare Robert had backed in the Miner's Cup had failed in the last few bounds to hold her lead over the favourite.

She could have turned two hundred pounds into two thousand. She had turned it into nothing, and Elizabeth could not feel any emotion whatever.

They simply never spoke of it.

John Trent helped to give Elizabeth strength to get through the first terrible days. It wasn't possible to know how much his quiet friendship helped Robert, but Elizabeth wondered sometimes what she would have done without him.

John handled funeral arrangements. John knew someone sailing for England who could be entrusted with letters for

Elizabeth's and Robert's families, telling them of Edward's death.

John never fussed, he never obtruded. But, warm and dependable as sunrise, he was somehow simply *there*, to be relied on and trusted.

Others were kind also. Elizabeth especially valued her friendship with Maggie Doyle.

Bert Peters came around to the Waldens' shack one evening to find Elizabeth standing outside looking at the western sky where the newly-set sun had turned a flecked sheaf of tiny clouds into brilliant beauty.

He touched his hat. "I don't want to intrude, Mrs Walden. I came to ask how you all are. And I brought this for Sarah."

He held out a hand-whittled wooden doll.

"I used to be quite good at making these, but I'm afraid I'm a bit out of practice."

"Why, it's very kind of you, Bert, and Sarah will love it. I must find some scraps of cloth and she can help me make clothes for the doll. It will be very good for her."

She glanced toward the hut where the gleam of a candle showed through a chink in the window.

"Robert is reading to her. I think it helps Sarah. Maybe it helps Robert, too."

She gave a little shiver and pulled her shawl more closely around her shoulders. "He needs help, Bert. I'm most terribly worried about him."

It was the first time she had admitted it to anyone; strange, she thought afterwards, that it should have been Bert she confided in.

Bert looked at her. "I should think you must be just as sad as Robert, Mrs Walden – more, if anything."

She put a hand for a moment to her throat as if it hurt her, and nodded numbly.

"It isn't just grief with Robert, Bert. It's – uglier than that. The grief is bad enough for all of us, but for Robert there's anger as well. The whole thing is like a black wall around him that no one can break through."

"He still blames Doc Miller?"

"I think so. He never talks about it. Oh, I know it will come right with time, because in time, when he's able to think reasonably again, he'll realize that even if Dr Miller hadn't been drunk, there was –" Her voice broke for a second and then she finished steadily, "There was almost certainly nothing that could have saved Edward. Robert will see that, in time."

She turned and faced Bert. "But he can't think reasonably yet. He's still shocked – ill with shock."

She hesitated. "Bert, would you try to coax him to go out with you? Persuade him to go to Maggie's place – play cards – I can give him a little money. I usually keep some put away. Would you try?"

Bert scratched his head. "It'll raise a few eyebrows," he said drily, "if word gets around that Robert Walden is out gambling a week or so after his son's death."

"I'm not concerned about raised eyebrows," Elizabeth said vehemently. "I'm only concerned about Robert. And he frightens me, Bert. There's something about him that frightens me."

Bert hesitated and then nodded. "All right. I'll try."

Elizabeth let him go into the house alone to talk to Robert, and when she went in after ten minutes she found Robert sitting at the table with Sarah asleep on his lap while he talked with Bert.

Bert looked around as Elizabeth came in. "I've been trying to persuade Robert to come and have a drink and play cards, Mrs Walden."

"I think that's a good idea," Elizabeth agreed.

Robert stared. "You do? But Elizabeth –"

She stepped up behind him and put her hands on his shoulders. "I know. But Robert, we have to go on living. Life is a perpetual challenge. We have to take it up, even when we don't want to; even when it means learning to *want* to live all over again."

She went into the bedroom and came back with his coat and handed it to him. "There's some money in your coat pocket. Not much, but enough."

She took the sleeping Sarah from him and smiled at him, and he went out with Bert reluctantly, almost as if he didn't know where he was going.

Several men turned their heads sharply when Bert and Robert walked into Maggie Doyle's saloon. Bert bought a bottle of whisky and he and Robert sat at a table and began to play cards. Robert was silent and seemed unable to concentrate, and when Bert cheerfully invited two strangers to join in four-handed poker he merely nodded absently.

But gradually he began to relax with the game and the whisky, and some of the haggardness eased out of his face as the old fascination of the cards began to slowly assert itself.

Then Dr Miller came in and went up to the bar and began drinking brandy and talking to the man next to him, not noticing Robert.

Robert had glanced up casually as the doctor came in and though he said nothing and appeared to turn his attention at once back to the cards, his face froze into blankness and he fell morosely silent. Time and again his hand reached out for the whisky bottle, and when it was empty he got up and bought another without a glance in Dr Miller's direction.

Bert watched Robert uneasily and most of the men in the bar, knowing the bitterness of Robert's attitude to Dr

Miller, kept a knot of drinkers around Miller so that he wouldn't see Robert.

But presently he did, and came over to the table. He held out his hand and said, "Hello, Robert. How are you? How's Mrs Walden?"

Robert never moved his eyes from his cards. "If anyone happens to see that broken-down drunk called Miller, tell him to stay out of my way."

There was an uneasy hush over the saloon. One man said, "Steady, Walden. The doctor meant well."

"Doctor!" Robert said it as if the word were some ugly blasphemy. "He's a dirty, sodden has-been, thrown out of every town he's been in."

There was a silence that seemed agonizingly long, and then Abraham Miller put down his glass, turned on his heel and walked out without a word.

"Robert," Bert Peters began, "there's —"

"It's your bid," Robert said.

Bert hesitated, then nodded and took up the cards again. The two strangers seemed puzzled and uncomfortable and presently withdrew.

Bert looked at Robert. "Do you want to turn it in?"

"No." Robert poured himself another drink and pushed the bottle toward Bert.

Bert shook his head. "No thanks. I've had enough, and so have you."

"If you don't like my habits," Robert said without looking up, "you should go home."

Bert stayed for another hour, but his efforts at conversation seemed to fall on deaf ears. Robert appeared totally absorbed in the cards, but Bert was aware — as was everyone in the saloon — that though Robert Walden's body sat at a table and played cards, his mind was somewhere else, in some black and private place.

Finally Bert put down his cards and yawned. "Well,

that's enough for me. Suppose I walk home with you?''

"I won't," Robert said flatly, "get lost."

"Maybe not. But you're not as sober as you might be."

"And I intend to get much drunker."

"Robert —"

"Leave me alone." The words were quiet and carefully spaced, and utterly final.

Bert Peters met Maggie Doyle's eyes across the bar and he raised his shoulders in a helpless shrug, said goodnight, and left.

Robert reached for the whisky bottle again.

It was very late when Elizabeth heard him come in — though, later, she could not say even approximately what time it might have been. She had been lying awake, waiting for the sound of his step and wondering whether her idea of getting him to go out with Bert had been right or wrong; and the night hours had stretched into unguessable time.

He had been drinking too much, she knew, because his step was too heavy. But he was steady on his feet and he didn't fumble in latching the door. She didn't want him to know she had been lying awake keeping watch for him, so she lay quietly pretending sleep.

He sat on the side of the bed and pulled his boots off. He didn't light the candle, but seemed to be able to find his way by the faint ghost of light that came through a window chink from the brilliance outdoors of a nearly-full moon.

He sat slumped for a while, and then lay back on the bed fully clothed, like a man too weary or too stupefied to undress, and was instantly asleep.

The night was sharp with a chill of late frost and Elizabeth got up quietly and carefully spread a blanket over him. At least, she thought gratefully as she slipped back to bed, he could get some peace while he slept.

She couldn't be sure, in retrospect, whether she had been

asleep or only dozing, when Sarah was suddenly beside her, shaking her.

"Mummy, Mummy! There's a fire – I think there's a house burning!"

Elizabeth scrambled quickly out of bed and pushed open the shutter. The harsh glow of fire flung itself redly into the sky, and she could see it was indeed a house burning.

"That's Dr Miller's house – I'm sure of it," she told Sarah.

Dr Miller's house stood a little isolated from the main part of the town and not far from the Waldens' hut.

Elizabeth shook Robert by the shoulder until he grunted protestingly and rolled over.

"Robert, quickly! There's a house on fire! Someone may need help."

He sat up, rubbing the back of his neck and pulling on his boots. He seemed only semi-conscious, but he stumbled outside and the sharp light of the fire seemed to jolt him awake and he set off at a run.

Elizabeth dressed and pulled on a woollen cloak and put a coat on Sarah and buttoned on their boots. Then, taking Sarah by the hand, she ran toward the fire, lighted over the rough ground by the moon and the cruel glare of the fire. Though she hadn't paused to think why, she was afraid.

Long before she reached the fire she could see that her first thought had been correct: it was Abraham Miller's house. It was burning fiercely, the heat too savage for anyone to get close, and as she and Sarah stopped, Robert came around from the far side of the building, shielding his face from the heat with his hands.

"It's no use," he said. "I can't get close enough even to look in."

"Dr Miller!" Elizabeth said hoarsely. "Why isn't he here?"

"Don't worry about him," Robert said. "Someone was

running away just as I got here, heading for the main town. It must have been Miller going for help. Though what anyone could do about putting that out is beyond me."

They turned at the sound of running footsteps. Two policemen came panting up, one still buttoning his coat. Half a dozen more men were close behind them.

"Nothing we can do about that," the sergeant said, staring at the burning house. He looked at Robert. "How long have you been here, Captain Walden?"

Robert shrugged. "Ten minutes. Fifteen, maybe. It was well alight when I got here."

Someone in the growing crowd of hastily-dressed onlookers said, "Where's Dr Miller?"

"Gone to raise the alarm, I should think," Robert answered. "Someone was running off into town when I arrived."

"Did Dr Miller alert you?" Elizabeth asked the police sergeant.

"No, Ma'am. Mr Trent reported the fire to us."

"Why did he go to you instead of to the fire-brigade?"

Elizabeth was never sure why she asked that question. She only knew that some strange, unnamed fear was clutching her.

The sergeant hesitated, continuing to stare at the flames.

"Because, Ma'am," he said slowly, "he thought he had managed to put out the fire, which hadn't got a very good hold when he saw it. It appears it must have flared up again."

"But why did he go to the police?" Elizabeth persisted.

Some of her uneasiness seemed to spread to the onlookers, for suddenly they fell silent and everyone looked at the police sergeant, waiting.

It was John Trent himself who answered. He had pushed his way through the knot of people and stood white-faced in the glare of the fire, shocked eyes on the blazing building. His left arm, heavy with plaster of Paris, hung in a sling, but it was clearly more than pain that caused the frozen look of his face.

"I didn't call the fire-brigade," he said, "because I thought I'd managed to put the fire out. It was dying down when I broke in. The bed and the curtains and some clothes were on fire, but the fire hadn't caught on the timber of the building. Or so I thought."

He paused and ran his tongue over his lips as if they were too dry to allow him to speak.

"I went to the police because when I broke in I found Dr Miller dead."

Seven

The magistrate's inquiry into the death of Abraham Miller followed a fortnight later.

It had been a fortnight of waking nightmare for Elizabeth. A fortnight when the police made interminable visits, asking interminably:

"Captain Walden, at what time did you leave the 'Wild Swan' hotel?"

"I don't know. I was rather drunk. Ask Maggie Doyle."

"When did you arrive home?"

"I don't know. Ten minutes after leaving the 'Wild Swan', I suppose. No, maybe a bit more."

"What did you do after you left the 'Wild Swan'?"

"I came home. That's all."

"Did you meet anyone on your way home?"

"No, I don't believe so."

"When did you last see Dr Miller?"

"On the night he died. He was in the 'Wild Swan'."

"Did you see him again later?"

"No."

"You were heard to insult him and warn him to keep out of your way. Is that correct?"

"Yes."

"You had previously been heard to threaten to kill him. Is that also correct?"

"Yes. But I didn't set fire to his house. If I wanted to kill a man, that's not the way I'd go about it."

"Even if you were drunk?"

"Even so."

He answered patiently, doggedly determined, it seemed, not to be aroused to anger by the suspicion that lay on him.

The police asked Elizabeth, again and again, what time Robert had come home. She could only answer that she didn't know.

"Mrs Walden, when your little girl called you to tell you there was a house on fire, how long was that after your husband came in?"

"I don't know."

"You must have some idea, though. Fifteen minutes? Half an hour?"

"I don't know, because I can't be sure whether or not I had fallen asleep. If I hadn't, then it was probably fifteen minutes after my husband came in. If I had been asleep, then I have no idea."

"How long would your husband have been at the scene of the fire before you arrived?"

"I should think about a quarter of an hour. I had to get both Sarah and myself into some clothes before we followed."

"Between leaving your house and arriving at Dr Miller's house, could you see the fire at all times?"

"No. For part of the way it would be out of sight because of a dip in the ground."

They know that, she thought; why are they trying to trap me?

"So that between the time you first saw the fire when your daughter roused you, and the time you arrived at the scene, the fire could have died down and then blazed up again?"

"It could have died down and blazed up again between the time I first saw it and the time I left the house. Not after that. I could see the glow."

And so the questions went on.

They were asked again at the Coroner's Court convened in the little weatherboard Courthouse, jammed with the interested and the curious on a clear early spring day.

Watching Robert give his evidence, stone-faced, Elizabeth felt even farther from him than in the other grim weeks since Edward died. This man she had lived with for ten years had become a stranger, possessed of deep-lying characteristics she had never guessed.

But when they put her in the witness chair and asked their questions about times and moods she ended her evidence by saying quietly to the magistrate:

"Your Honour, there are many things I do not know, such as when my husband came in on the night in question. But there is one thing I do know."

She turned to meet Robert's eyes.

"My husband did not kill Dr Miller. He could never plan to kill a man by setting fire to his house. Such a thing would be monstrously cruel, and Robert Walden could never be deliberately cruel."

There was a stillness in the packed room, and Robert's dark eyes, fixed on his wife, lit in a slow smile.

The magistrate cleared his throat. "Your husband is not on trial, Mrs Walden," he said, not ungently. "He has been accused of nothing. The sole purpose of this Court is to try to establish the facts which led up to the death of Dr Abraham Miller."

John Trent was the next witness.

Asked to tell the Court what had happened on the night in question, he explained that he had been working late at the store and, as he was leaving to retire to his quarters – a small separate building at the back of the store – in the moonlight he misjudged the stairs at the front of the store, stumbled and fell.

"My left wrist hurt badly and I suspected I'd broken it, so I went to Dr Miller's house."

"What time was that, Mr Trent?" the magistrate asked.

"Just about eleven. I knew Dr Miller was still up, because I could see the light of a candle through the curtains. He came to the door and told me to get out, it was eleven at night and he'd had enough of dirty insulting miners for one day."

"Did Dr Miller appear sober?"

"I noticed he was slightly unsteady on his feet. I'd never seen him in such ill temper. Usually he's a most cheerful man. Then he recognized me and said, 'Oh, it's you, young John. Good Lord, that wrist's broken. Well, you'd better come in.' And he took me in and set my wrist."

"So he was in fact not drunk."

John hesitated, his face serious. "I would say he was not sober," he answered. "But Dr Miller was a very skilful doctor and he would have to be very drunk indeed before he wasn't able to do anything so routine as setting a simple fracture. He smelt of brandy and there was a brandy bottle on the table. I don't know how much was in it."

"Where was the candle?"

"On the table beside the bottle."

"What did you do after the doctor had attended to your wrist?"

"I went home. Dr Miller shut the door behind me, saying he wasn't going to open it again to anyone. I went to bed, but I wasn't able to sleep for the pain in my wrist, so I got up again and went for a walk in the moonlight. That's when I saw the fire. At first it didn't occur to me it was a building alight, but I was curious and started walking toward it. When I got close I saw it was Dr Miller's house."

"Why didn't you raise the alarm at once, Mr Trent?"

John shook his head. "I wish now that I had, but at the time my only thought was that Dr Miller might well still be in the house, asleep. The fire didn't seem to have any more than just started, so I felt I could get in if I hurried. I was much closer to the house than to the main part of town by then. There wasn't anyone about as far as I could see, and there are no other houses very close, so it seemed to me the best thing I could do was get to the doctor's house as fast as possible."

He paused, and added, "From what I'd seen of him an hour earlier, I felt he might well have drunk so much he'd be much too heavily asleep for the fire to waken him. Anyway, I believe a sleeping person often isn't wakened by fire – at least not in time to escape."

The magistrate said, "I'm sure everyone would agree that your action was correct, Mr Trent. Indeed, if I may say so, I think you acted with courage. Please go on."

John's fair skin coloured slightly. "It wasn't a matter of courage, sir. I just did the first thing that came into my head. The door wasn't locked or bolted, so I just pushed it open. There was a lot of smoke, and I could see the curtains were on fire, and the bedclothes, and also some clothes lying on the floor. I got my coat off – I only had it half on, anyway, because of having my arm in a sling – and I was able to beat the flames out with it. First I put out the fire on Dr Miller's clothes. I thought he might be just unconscious."

"Was he fully dressed or had he prepared for bed?"

John thought for a moment. "His clothes had been fairly badly burned, and in the stress of the moment I didn't particularly notice. I believe he was barefooted, but I'm fairly sure he was wearing trousers – possibly pulled on over his nightclothes, as if he had partly dressed on being wakened by the fire."

He frowned. "That would mean he knew about the fire and had time to partly dress and yet was overcome by smoke. I don't know, sir," he said uneasily. "It's just guesswork."

"You feel that, since you could put the fire out with only one good hand – and somewhat at a later stage of its development, Dr Miller should have had no difficulty in putting it out or at least escaping from the building?"

"That thought did occur to me, sir, yes."

"And having put the fire out, you examined Dr Miller more closely?"

"Yes. Because I had the use of only one arm, I had to put the fire out first, instead of getting Dr Miller outside first. But when I examined him, even though now I had no light but the moonlight through the window, I saw quite clearly he was dead."

"There was no doubt of that?"

"No, sir, no doubt whatever."

"So, believing the fire out, you left and went for the police?"

"Yes. I was quite certain the fire was out, but unfortunately something must have been smouldering still, and flared up when I left."

"Mr Trent, did you notice the deceased's candle-holder while you were in the room during or after the fire?"

"Yes. It was lying on the floor beside the bed. The doctor must have dropped it or knocked it over and it set fire to the bedclothes."

"I see." The magistrate pushed his glasses back into place on the bridge of his nose. "You mentioned that, in addition to the bedclothes, the curtains and some clothes were alight. Where were the clothes?''

"Well, more or less in a heap against the wall.''

"So three separate items in the room were burning: the bedclothes, the curtains, and a pile of clothing against the wall?''

John's eyes narrowed with caution and concentration as he saw where the question was leading.

"Yes,'' he said.

"And yet you said the actual floor and wall timbers had not caught fire?''

"They didn't appear to have, no.''

"Doesn't it seem rather strange to you that three separate lots of combustible material were on fire in different parts of the room, even though the floor and walls were not burning?''

The courtroom was very silent.

John Trent said slowly, "I'm not expert in the matter of how a fire like that could spread.''

The magistrate thanked him and told him he might stand down.

Sergeant Clarence Emery was called and he told how he had been wakened by Mr John Trent after midnight on the night in question and told that Mr Trent had found Dr Miller dead in his burning house. He – Sergeant Emery – had hastily dressed and, together with one of his men, had gone to Dr Miller's house, only to find it a mass of flame. The firebrigade had arrived later – volunteer firemen with horse-drawn equipment – but there was little anyone could do that night.

"Next morning,'' the sergeant went on routinely, "when the ruins of the building were cool enough, I searched them with the aid of my men. I found a fire-damaged brandy-bottle beside the remains of the iron bedstead, and also a candle-holder. We recovered the badly-burned body of Dr

Miller, which was lying on the remains of the bed."

John Trent had been sitting with his legs stretched out in front of him, studying the toes of his boots with apparent interest. Now his head jerked up and he came instinctively to his feet.

"But the body wasn't on the bed!" he said sharply.

Everyone in the courtroom turned to look at him.

"I assure you, sir," Sergeant Emery said, "it *was* lying on the bed. It was an iron bedstead with a wire mesh mattress-base and so, although the mattress and bedclothes were virtually destroyed, the entire framework of the bed was intact. The body was lying on it. You can ask the men who were assisting in the task of searching the ruins."

John stood for a long moment in silence. Then he said, "I'm sorry. In the distress of the moment I obviously became confused over the details. Yes, I believe you're quite correct. The body was on the bed, of course."

He sat down quickly, and there was a little rippling murmur of speculation, which the magistrate silenced.

"Were you able," the magistrate asked the police officer, "to determine the cause of the fire?"

"No, Your Honour. It appeared probable from the position of the candle-holder that the deceased had dropped the candle or knocked it over, starting the fire by setting the bedclothes alight."

"You heard Mr Trent's evidence. Do you feel it likely that three separate items in different parts of the room could have been accidentally ignited from the one source?"

The policeman shook his head. "I can't answer that with any certainty, sir. It seems unlikely; and yet fire is such an unpredictable thing I couldn't say it wouldn't happen, since I didn't see the particular circumstances myself."

"Were you able to ascertain whether or not the deceased was dressed?"

Why do they keep asking that? Elizabeth wondered.

"Yes, sir. In that instance Mr Trent's memory served him correctly. Although the clothing was all but destroyed, we were able to tell from cloth fragments that Dr Miller was bare-footed and had put on a pair of trousers over his nightshirt."

"Thus suggesting he was aroused by the fire and was preparing to leave the building when he was overcome?"

"It could suggest that, sir, yes. It could also suggest that someone came to the door after Dr Miller had gone to bed and the doctor got up to admit that person. But that is pure conjecture, of course. A number of reasons for his being partly dressed could be advanced. All we know is that he had prepared for bed and then put on a pair of trousers. Because of the position of the body, lying on the bed, it would seem that, having partly dressed, Dr Miller had in fact gone to bed."

Much of the tension went out of the atmosphere of the packed courtroom with the end of the police sergeant's evidence.

It seemed the whole thing would fizzle out in a "death by misadventure" finding.

But the sensations were not quite over.

No one displayed much interest when Dr Herman Baker was called. Another of the town's doctors, he was much younger than Dr Miller and had an air of competent professionalism.

He told the court that he, in compliance with a police request and in accordance with his duty as Government surgeon, had carried out a post mortem examination of the body of Abraham Miller.

"Were you," the magistrate asked, "able to determine the cause of death?"

"I was."

"In spite of the fact the body had been severely burned?"

"Even so, it did not conceal the cause of death. The deceased was killed by massive brain damage resulting from a severe fracture of the skull. He had been struck a violent blow from behind with some heavy object. Death would have been virtually instantaneous."

A wave of shocked and excited comment rose and broke over the courtroom.

The magistrate demanded order – and got it, Elizabeth felt through her own sense of shock, only because the people wanted to hear what else the doctor had to say.

The magistrate looked hard at Dr Baker. "Are you certain the injury could not have been caused accidentally – for example, by the deceased falling and striking his head?"

"By the nature and position of the wound, no."

"Could part of the burning building not have collapsed on the doctor, causing the injury?"

"Again, no. I was in fact present when the police recovered the body. The injury could not have been caused by falling ruins. This, again, I judge by the nature and position of the injury, and by the position of the ruined timbers in relation to the body. The body was face-up on the bed, and any injury caused by collapsing parts of the building would have been to the front part of the head."

"You are saying that Dr Abraham Miller was murdered?"

"Yes. He was murdered. He was dead before the fire touched him."

Eight

Elizabeth took Robert's arm as they walked out of the courtroom into the warm sun of the brilliant spring day that suddenly felt bleak.

She took his arm in defiance of the stares and the silence that greeted them. Head erect, she was wordlessly telling the world that her faith in this man was unshakeable.

No one could guess that she was numb with a fearful coldness no sun could warm. Her clear grey eyes smiled a greeting to people she knew, and no one could guess that she was almost unseeing with shock.

No one spoke. The people who had jammed the courtroom and heard the magistrate's finding of murder by a person or persons unknown now stood in a sullen group outside, making a path for the Waldens to pass. But somehow even the fact that they stood back to let them go by held more than a hint of menace.

Elizabeth managed to keep her voice steady enough to say, "Good afternoon," to several people, as pleasantly as if she never dreamed there was any suggestion of antagonism.

No one answered, except John Trent, who instantly raised his hat and said, "Good afternoon, Mrs Walden; Robert."

His eyes met Elizabeth's for a moment, and she saw a profound pity in them which shook her more than the crowd's hostility.

She and Robert didn't exchange a word until they were back in their cabin.

Robert swept off his hat and hung it up, and then looked down at her and took her by the shoulders and kissed her gently.

"Thank you, my Elizabeth," he said with a little smile.

She shivered. "Oh, Robert, what shall we do?"

"Do?" His dark eyebrows shot up.

"Everyone – suspects you."

"Let 'em." He took a whisky bottle off a high shelf and poured two stiff drinks. "Have this, my dear. You must need it."

She sipped it cautiously, grateful for its warmth spreading through her. Presently she raised her eyes to his face.

"But Robert, Dr Miller was murdered. Why should anyone want to kill him?"

"Anyone except Robert Walden? Quite so. But while I have no alibi, neither does anyone have a shred of evidence against me. They can think what they choose. They can't touch me."

He downed his whisky and poured himself another.

"Better go and get Sarah," he suggested, hanging up his coat and pulling off his white shirt.

"What are you going to do?" Elizabeth asked.

"Oh, may as well go down the shaft for a couple of hours."

He folded his grey trousers, pausing for the briefest of moments to look at the very faint marks where all Elizabeth's efforts had not been able to completely remove the bloodstains from race-day.

"How soon can we leave?" asked Elizabeth.

"Leave for where?"

"I don't know. Anywhere. Robert, we must leave Gympie!"

He tucked his grey flannel shirt into his work-trousers and turned to look at her. "Abraham Miller," he said flatly, "is not going to drive me anywhere." And he picked up his hat and went out.

Elizabeth stood for a long time, her hands over her face. Finally she walked slowly to the door. She must go and get Sarah.

Sarah had gone to spend the day with the Anglican clergyman's wife. The Reverend and Mrs Alfred Moore had two small daughters – one the same age as Sarah and one a couple of years older – and the three children were good friends. When word had spread that Elizabeth was teaching Sarah and Edward, a number of parents had asked if she would teach their children also, because many of the people on the field had no books and school facilities were quite inadequate. So Elizabeth had had about a dozen children at her informal classes, and the Moores' daughters had been among them.

Elizabeth began to walk toward the centre of the town, but she knew she would not go first to the Moores' house. There was something she didn't want to know, but had to know.

Over and over her mind heard Robert say: "I didn't set fire to his house. If I wanted to kill a man, that's not the way I'd go about it." She heard her own voice declaring, "My husband did not kill Dr Miller. He could never plan to kill a man by setting fire to his house."

But whoever had killed Dr Miller had not used fire to kill. Whoever the murderer was, he had killed with a powerful blow. The kind of blow that might be driven by hate, or unbearable anger.

Fire had been meant to conceal the truth, to allow the whole thing to be regarded as an accident brought about by the doctor's drunken state.

"Robert Walden could not kill a man by fire," she said aloud.

The thing that clutched her with the terrible claws of dread was the fact that she could not make herself repeat the sentence, leaving out the last two words.

She found John Trent at work in his store, discussing the merits of a particular saddle as against another saddle. He looked up as she came in, as if he had been expecting her.

"May I help you, Mrs Walden?"

"I should like to see you privately, Mr Trent, when you're free."

He nodded and asked his customer to excuse him, calling one of his sales clerks to take over the saddlery discussion. "Perhaps you'd step into my office?" he asked Elizabeth.

He shut the door of the small room behind them and gestured to the only chair, which he drew out from the invoice-littered desk. He sat on a packing case which seemed to be there to do duty as an extra chair.

His blue eyes met hers steadily.

"If it will make it easier," he said quietly, "I can guess why you've come. You want to ask me about what I said in the courtroom today, when I interrupted the police sergeant to say the body was not on the bed."

"Yes," she said.

"But, Mrs Walden, you must recall that I later withdrew the remark and agreed that the body had been on the bed."

"I know. But I didn't believe you."

"I'm not in the habit of telling lies."

She smiled faintly. "Perhaps that's why you're not very good at it." Her hand on the desk clenched quickly. "Please, I must know. I must know!"

He looked at her for a full minute, and then nodded. "Very well. When I broke into Dr Miller's house that night and beat the fire out, and found him, he was lying dead on the floor with his legs partly under the bed."

"I see." There was a little silence. "And as far as we know, Robert was next on the scene."

He nodded. "I'm sorry. The moment I said what I did about the body being on the floor, I realized what I'd done and withdrew my remark."

"You think Robert, when he got there ahead of Sarah and me, put the body on the bed and re-started the fire?"

"I don't know."

"But it's what you think, isn't it?" she demanded.

John shook his head. "I only know the body was on the floor and the fire apparently out when I left. Obviously within a few minutes the fire sprang up again, and I suspect it didn't do so of its own accord. And *someone* put the body back on the bed so the police would find it there next morning, and the fire and Dr Miller's death would have a better chance of being put down to accident. Someone went into the house after I left. Whoever it was, it must have been the person who murdered Miller."

And there was precious little opportunity for anyone other than Robert to do it.

Neither spoke the words, but they hung there in the silence no less strongly.

She said after a few moments, "People will still believe Robert guilty, even though you never tell a soul what you know."

His eyes were on her face, and there was only kindness in them. "I'm afraid so. But they have no evidence."

"That," she said with a touch of bitterness, "is what Robert said. He seemed to think that was all that mattered."

John said slowly, "Well, I suppose it is, in the long run. Without evidence the law can't touch him, and the story isn't likely to follow him and spoil his chances of a new beginning."

"No," Elizabeth agreed wryly. "It won't. He isn't going anywhere for the story to follow."

John stared. "But he must!"

He made a quick gesture. "I'm sorry. I have no right to tell you or your husband what you should do."

She smiled. "It's all right."

He jammed his hands into his trouser-pockets. "It's just – I'm afraid people might make life unpleasant for you. Dr Miller was very well liked – and deservedly so. He was a kind man. People could be unpleasant to you."

"Robert may give in, in time," Elizabeth said without conviction. "Meanwhile, we shall just have to accept being outcasts."

She looked at him. "The police will ask you again about the position of the body."

"And I shall tell them again I made a mistake. It was on the bed. And they'll go on having no kind of evidence against Robert.

"What if they *did* know that someone had gone into Dr Miller's house after you left?"

He said carefully, "They couldn't prove it was Robert."

"But they would say," she said slowly, as if the words forced themselves out against her will, " 'Who else would it have been?' They would say that, wouldn't they?"

He didn't answer.

"It – doesn't look very good for Robert, does it?" she said in a low voice.

He was silent for a moment. "Mrs Walden, do you think Robert killed Dr Miller?"

"No!" she said sharply, raising her head to look at him.

He met her gaze for a little while and then she stood up
and turned away from him.

"Oh, God," she whispered. "If only I could be sure."

She ran her fingers along the edge of the desk-top,
carefully feeling its texture, and not even knowing it was
there.

"I knew he hadn't killed him by setting fire to the
house," she said dully. "Even though I've been afraid ever
since the fire, afraid of finding the truth, I always knew
Robert hadn't killed him by setting fire to the house. But
Dr Miller wasn't killed by anyone setting fire to his house."

She took a long breath. "I must go and get Sarah. It will
be hardest for Sarah if the town turns against us. She's too
young to understand why."

John had got to his feet to open the door for her, and he
looked down at her with compassion. "I wish I could help."

"You have helped a great deal." She looked up at him
and smiled faintly. "You may have saved us all from seeing
Robert put on trial –"

Her voice broke on the word and he put an arm
protectively about her shoulders. She put her face against
his chest and for a second his arms tightened around her.

Then she stood straight and he let her go. "You're very
kind," she said, in control of her voice again. "Thank you."

He opened the door and she went out. He stood and
watched her until she had gone out of the store.

Mrs Edna Baker, the handsome wife of the doctor who a
few hours earlier had given evidence of the cause of Dr
Miller's death, was visiting at the cabin beside the Anglican
Church which served the Moores as a vicarage, when
Elizabeth arrived to take Sarah home.

She smiled at Elizabeth without warmth while Mrs
Moore looked flustered and said she would get Sarah.

Mrs Baker said, "I'm glad you've come, Mrs Walden. I was going to send a message, but now I can deliver it in person. You'll remember I asked you to tea next Thursday. Unfortunately I find I have to cancel the invitation. Thursday is unsuitable, as it turns out."

Elizabeth smiled politely. "That's perfectly all right, Mrs Baker. Perhaps another time."

"Of course." The tone made it quite clear there would be no other time. "But I suppose you and your husband will be leaving quite soon."

"Leaving?" Elizabeth looked surprised. "Oh, I shouldn't think so. Robert doesn't feel he's fully explored the potential of his claim yet." She smiled. "My husband is an incurable optimist."

"Really." Mrs Baker paused as Mrs Moore came in with her two daughters and Sarah.

Sarah ran to her mother, eyes dancing. "Mummy, I've been playing with Miranda's doll. She's ever so pretty and we've been playing houses and Miranda's going to let me play with her doll again because she's going to bring it to our place when we have lessons again tomorrow."

Watching the outgoing enthusiasm for life that sparkled in her eyes, so like her father's, Elizabeth smiled. "That's nice, darling."

Mrs Baker said: "Mrs Moore was just saying she thought her little girls unfortunately wouldn't be able to attend your classes any more, Mrs Walden."

"Oh," Elizabeth said. "I see."

Mrs Moore looked uncomfortable. "Well, nothing's definite, Mrs Walden. It will – we're not sure – nothing's been decided. It will all depend on my husband."

"That's quite all right," Elizabeth said pleasantly. "Come along, Sarah. Thank you for taking care of her, Mrs Moore. I'm sorry to have had to inconvenience you."

"Oh, it wasn't any inconvenience, Mrs Walden," the clergyman's wife said anxiously. "I'm glad to help and Sarah's a dear little girl and no bother."

"You're a kind-hearted woman, Mrs Moore," Mrs Baker said firmly, "but it is a fact that people do impose on clergyman's wives."

"Good afternoon, ladies," Elizabeth said, taking Sarah's hand.

She had just stepped outside when the whistle began to blow – a long, deep hoot of steam-driven sound from one of the big mines. Elizabeth was so full of hurt that for a few seconds the sound didn't reach her mind.

It went on and on, and she halted her step instinctively. "What's that?" she demanded sharply.

People were beginning to run, and voices in the distance were raised.

Both the other women had come to the door, their eyes turned toward the source of the sound.

"It's the warning whistle," Mrs Moore answered. "There's been an accident in one of the mines."

Elizabeth's eyes widened in horror. Many men worked underground in the big mines. She had seen the iron lift-cages full of men being lowered down the shaft at the beginning of a new shift, while the men from the previous shift who had ridden up in the cages streamed out of the mine entrances, weary and filthy, almost unrecognisable under a thick layer of sweat-streaked dust.

As in any underground mine, they worked always with the chance that a rock-fall or a premature explosion could kill them in an instant; or – far worse – trap them behind a wall of rock-rubble in a pocket of diminishing air. It was part of the price of gold; and, in this case, someone else's gold.

"I think it must have been in the Southern Colonial,"

Mrs Baker said, and the three women stood for a minute, looking toward the mine-head, momentarily united in shock, even though none of them had a husband down the mine.

"I must go home," Elizabeth said finally, as much to herself as anyone. She must go home and resist the urge to go to the mine. The crowd already would be big enough to hamper those whose job it was to handle rescue attempts.

Yet those who went were not ghouls, she reflected; even those who had neither relatives nor friends to fear for. They went because they felt a sense of involvement, a need to know what was happening.

It was Bert Peters who brought the Waldens the news of what had happened. Elizabeth had forgotten that Bert sometimes worked down the mine.

"You remember pulling old Tom Sanderson out of the way of that bolting horse," he said to Elizabeth. "Well, Tom worked at the mine, odd jobs, mostly – anything where it didn't matter that he was as deaf as a stone. Always the mines people made sure it was surface work, though; he never went underground. But today a man he knew was sick and couldn't go down, so Tom said he'd take his place, and so he did. He'd had a lot of experience underground back in England before he lost his hearing. He didn't hear the warning signal that a charge had been set, and the others on the shift forgot for the moment he was deaf.

"He walked nearly up to the charge. One of the other men made a dash for him to try to get him away before the charge went off, but there wasn't time. There was a lot of flying rock and poor old Tom was killed outright. The other man got his leg broken and was trapped for a while by rock; it's a miracle he wasn't killed. They didn't know at first how many men were involved and so sounded the general accident alarm."

Bert paused. "Tom had a little dog – nice little dog he called Sandy. Now it's got no one to look after it and I sort of wondered if you'd let Sarah have it. Be a playmate for her."

"Why, Bert, that's a kind thought," Elizabeth said. "I'd like her to have it. Robert?"

Robert nodded. "The children –" He stopped. "She's never had a pet. Might be a good idea."

And so Sandy came to live with the Waldens; and he *was* a good idea. Sarah eyed him at first with caution, and he surveyed his change of environment with bewilderment, but within twenty-four hours he was Sarah's devoted friend, and she was enchanted by him.

Sarah needed a friend, and as time went on she needed him more.

The police might have had no proof of the identity of Dr Miller's murderer, but the town had few doubts.

Abraham Miller had been an alcoholic and he had been unreliable, but he had brought a high level of medical ability to a crude mining town, and with it he had brought a generous nature. Many a miner down on his luck could tell how the tubby little doctor had stiched a cut or set a broken limb or removed an inflamed appendix, and forgotten to send a bill. Many a mother recalled how he had sat all night, if need be, with a sick child, or driven his horse and buggy through a storm along a rough bush track to attend a difficult confinement.

The doctor might not have suited the regularity or the nice manners of an orthodox practice. But in the harshness of a mining town where any medical help was greatly valued, Dr Miller had been loved.

People could understand Robert Walden's momentary bitterness, even though Dr Baker had agreed that it was extremely doubtful whether any doctor, however promptly on the scene, could have done anything to save Edward.

People could understand Robert's anger. But they could never forgive cold, calculating murder, and they made life hard for the Waldens.

The first Sunday morning after the enquiry, when the Waldens took their places in the little timber church, almost the entire congregation got up and walked out.

Sarah watched in bewilderment but said nothing as Elizabeth sat with her head bowed until the last footfall left the wooden floor. Then Elizabeth raised her head and touched Robert's arm.

"We must go out," she whispered.

"No," Robert said flatly.

"Robert —"

"No."

He sat with his arms folded, watching the vicar with a steel-glint in his dark eyes, silently challenging him.

The red-faced Mr Moore fussed with his sermon notes and finally conducted the service in the presence of his wife and two little daughters, the Waldens, and John Trent.

Afterwards, as they walked home, Sarah said, "Mummy, why did all the people walk out of church?"

Elizabeth hesitated. "Because they don't like us, I'm afraid, darling."

Sarah stared at her. "Why?"

Elizabeth stopped walking for a moment and looked down from the hill toward the river. How did you tell a six-year-old who nevertheless had a right to know the truth?

"You know Dr Miller died the night his house caught fire."

"Yes."

"Do you know that someone killed him and then set fire to his house to make it look like an accident?"

"Why did they kill Dr Miller? He was a nice man," Sarah declared, looking concerned.

Robert was looking off into the distance.

"Yes," Elizabeth said. "He was a nice man. We don't know why anyone would kill him." She took a quick breath. "People think Daddy killed him, Sarah. That's why they don't like us."

Sarah looked thoughtful for a minute. "That's silly," she said eventually.

Robert stooped and swung her up to ride on his shoulders. "I love you, princess," he said.

When they were back at the shack and Sarah's good dress had been changed and she had gone outside to play with Sandy, Elizabeth said: "Robert, we must leave."

"No," he said.

"But don't you see —"

"Yes, I do see!" he snapped. He whirled around to face her, his eyes blazing. "I see that if I run, it's an admission of guilt. And I'm damned if I'll give them that satisfaction!"

She turned away, and in a moment he went to her and put his hands gently on her shoulders.

"It's only for a little while. People will begin to forget. And as long as we stick it out they'll begin to think maybe they were wrong, after all. And anyway, it's not as if we'd be here forever. Win or lose at this gold game, we'll be moving on presently."

There was a little silence. "Yes," she said. "We'll be moving on."

He brushed his lips against her hair. "That's my Elizabeth." He began to change his clothes. "Why don't you start classes for the children again? You used to have a whole swarm of them coming when you gave our chil – when you gave Sarah lessons. Why don't you have them again? You started again a couple of weeks ago, but this week you've stopped. I meant to ask why, a few days ago."

"The answer's easy," she said quietly. "Since the fire not as many have come. And since the enquiry none come at all. I don't go around their parents to ask why."

He stood still for a moment, staring at her. Then he carefully hung up his tie.

"I see. Liz, why don't you and Sarah go out to stay with Jim and Molly Burton for a while? Give things a chance to settle down?"

She thought of the beauty of Oak Bend, and the comfortable homestead, and the freedom from stares that varied from curious to hostile.

Her chin lifted. "No," she said.

He smiled. "Thank you, my dear. I know that in the face of twenty witnesses swearing they'd seen me club Miller down, you'd still defy them. But to take Sarah out of this atmosphere for a while isn't running away. She's only a little girl. It's hardly fair on her."

Nine

Elizabeth and Sarah went to Oak Bend, but not until they had faced many more weeks of the town's hostility making itself clearer in a dozen small hurts. Robert withdrew more into himself and appeared completely unaware of people's attitudes. He worked at a furious pace, driving himself each day to exhaustion as if fighting against allowing himself to think.

Only once he was roused to a brief flare of anger when Sarah came home in tears from a former playmate's house and was eventually coaxed to tell Elizabeth what was wrong.

"Sam said Daddy was a murderer and he'd be hung one day," she sobbed. "What's a murderer?"

Robert, coming in at that moment, stopped in the doorway, his face darkening.

"In some cases," he said, "a murderer is a benefactor of mankind. Don't worry, princess, they aren't going to hang me, I promise. Suppose you and Sandy and I go for a walk?"

He whisked her off, and Elizabeth sank into a chair beside the pine table, and buried her face in her arms, too shaken even to cry.

She didn't see the shadow fall across the room as the man stepped to the doorway. Even his shocked cry of:

"Elizabeth!" didn't fully reach her thoughts.

Then suddenly John Trent was beside her, an arm strongly about her, saying urgently, "What is it? What's wrong? You're ill!"

She sat up, trying to focus her thoughts, pushing back a straying lock of hair from her face.

"No, no, I'm not ill. I'm sorry. I was just – just tired. I'm all right – truly I am."

He took his arm away and straightened up, sweeping off his hat, his honest face flushing.

"I do beg your pardon. I came to the door – it was open – and seeing you there, like that, I thought – I thought you were ill."

She shook her head. "I'm the one who should apologize. I was just being a wilting lily." She stood up. "Will you have some tea? The kettle's still on the boil, I see. It was chilly this morning and I put more wood on the fire."

She lifted the lid of the heavy iron kettle hanging by a hook and chain over the hearth. "Or," she added wryly, "would having tea at the Waldens' place turn you into an outcast, too? It might be bad for business."

A muscle tightened in his jaw. "I would have thought I put friendship ahead of business."

She half reached out a hand to him. "I'm sorry. That was unpardonable of me. You've been a wonderful friend, all these weeks since Edward died – and especially now. It would have been dreadful without you and Bert Peters. God knows we have few friends now."

There was a long run of silent seconds when she wasn't even aware of the silence, filled as it was with her thoughts. Then John said very quietly, "Please, sit down. I must talk to you."

When she had sat down, looking surprised at his tone, he said, "How much longer can you go on like this?"

"As long as I must."

"It will never change, as long as you live. Have you thought of that?"

"Oh, yes." Her tone was softly bitter. "You'd be surprised how much thinking you can do in a whole string of nights when you don't sleep."

He made an apologetic gesture. "Don't be angry with me. Believe me, I want to help."

She looked at him and some of the strain in her face lessened. "I know. I'm sorry I was ill-tempered. It's just that things get a little difficult sometimes."

He frowned. "I get so angry when I see the town being rude to you. Whatever it may think of Robert, it has no cause to turn on you."

"Even when I show them I believe in him?"

"Do you? Believe in him?"

"Of course."

"Do you?"

"Yes, yes, yes! How many times do I have to repeat it?"

"Then look at me when you say it. Do you believe in him?"

She leapt up. "Leave me alone! What right do you imagine you have to come here, badgering me? You call yourself a friend! You're no better than a pestering policeman or an interfering newspaperman. If that's your friendship I don't want it! Leave me alone!"

"I won't leave you alone to destroy yourself," he said steadily. "Because that's what you will do if you live the rest of your life with Robert Walden."

She was standing with her back to him, facing the wall. "I'm his wife."

"That doesn't give him the right to ruin your life. What kind of future do you have with him? He'll eternally rush from one adventure to the next, no matter how hair-brained each new fortune-making scheme may be. You'll be dragged along with him – in shacks like this one on some other goldfield, or in a tent while he helps build a railway, or on a smelly boat while he tries for wealth by pearling or he plans a wonderful new shipping run. That's the way it will always be."

"I know that."

"That's not the kind of life you want – not for yourself nor for Sarah. You know it and I know it. And it's not the kind of life you should have."

He paused. "That would be bad enough," he said, "if you were doing it for the man Robert was before Edward was killed. But now you will be doing it for a man suspected of murder."

"Stop it," she whispered.

"If it were just that the rest of the world suspected him of murder, even then it wouldn't be so bad. But you'll be doing it for a man *you* suspect of murder."

She clenched her hands. "Stop!"

"I won't stop, because you have to face the truth. I've watched you over these past few weeks. It's not the unkind things people do and say that make you lie awake at night till your eyes have dark circles under them and your face is haggard and you look like a haunted person."

He got up and stood behind her.

"It's because *you* think he's a murderer. That's the truth, isn't it?"

There was a long silence. Neither of them moved. The soft sound of the kettle singing on the fire was clearly audible in the stillness and, distantly, the growling of the crushing batteries.

Elizabeth shuddered. "I don't know. Oh, God, I don't know."

He didn't speak for a while. Then he said, "That's what I

meant when I said it will always be so, my dear. Not only must you face a life of wandering and insecurity. You have to face life – whatever kind of life the future may hold – with a man you cannot believe in any longer."

She stood straight and tall, with her back still turned to him. "I am his wife," she said again.

"And I say that isn't enough. He can see what the town is doing to you and to Sarah. But he puts his own pride first. He won't give in, no matter how much you get hurt."

Elizabeth said tautly, "Now I'll ask *you* a question. Do you *know* that Robert is a murderer?"

"No," John answered levelly. "I know no more than you do. But there is one thing I know that perhaps you don't."

She wheeled around to face him, her eyes wide with anxiety. "What?" she demanded.

"I love you."

She stared at him, not sure she had heard correctly. "What did you say?" she asked in bewilderment.

He took her hands in his. "I love you, Elizabeth. I love you. I can give you the kind of life you want – the kind of life you should have, you and Sarah both. My dear Elizabeth, don't let Robert destroy you."

She shook her head slowly as if to clear her mind. "I'm dreaming," she said. "This can't be happening."

"Oh, yes, it can."

"Are you asking me to leave Robert for you?"

"Yes." He smiled faintly. "Oh, my dear, I know you don't love me. But at least I can offer you a chance at life. I'm not by any means a poor man. I can take you far away from here, to any place you want to go, where no one knows anything about Robert Walden, no one would know you were not legally my wife. I can –"

"Please." She shook her head and took her hands from his. "Don't."

"Elizabeth, if Dr Miller hadn't been killed, I would never have asked you to do this. I'd have been more than a fool if I had, because I know what the answer would have been. But I've seen you lose your trust in Robert. What's left between people when trust is gone?"

She sat down slowly. "I have to think," she said dazedly. "What you're asking me to do – I can't absorb it. I've never once thought of leaving Robert – how could I?"

He nodded. "I know. I'll go now. But remember" – his eyes were earnest – "you can trust me. Always. Can you believe that?"

She looked at him and smiled faintly. "Yes. I believe I can."

She sat for a long time, looking at nothing, shocked, as much as anything, by the fact she had not flatly rejected John's offer. She knew why, if she was prepared to face the fact.

She had spoken the truth when she had said she had never considered leaving Robert. She had never considered it because she could not imagine how she and Sarah could physically survive in this country if she left Robert. She had been trained for nothing but being someone's wife. Now, shatteringly and against all her upbringing, John had offered her an escape. But was it simply exchanging one shame for another?

John, the kindly, pleasant friend. John the steady one, the one who was always there when he was needed. He always would be.

Trust. What's left between people when trust is gone? "I've seen you lose your trust in Robert." Robert. The gay, laughing, irresponsible, charming. The centre of her world in the eleven years since she had first met him; her king in the ten years since she had married him, known the ecstasy of being loved by him, the anxiety of never knowing what idea might seize him next, sometimes the misery and humiliation of knowing his gambling had rendered them penniless but for the small income she had from her family in England.

And always, always, she could forgive him anything.

Even murder?

She had to face that now, and find her own answer. It could not be an easy answer to find.

So it was with a sense of thankfulness that she went to Oak Bend, she and Sarah driving out with Jim Burton after one of his trips to town with farm produce to sell.

He said with concern that it would be a rough and slow trip. "I've only the dray I brought the pumpkins in, and the only cushion is a hessian bag stuffed with hay."

Elizabeth assured him it would be all right. She didn't tell him she would gladly have ridden in a dray much farther than the miles to Oak Bend in order to escape the atmosphere of the town for a while; to be away from Robert; to think.

Molly gave them a delighted welcome, took Elizabeth's hands and looked at her gravely for a minute and declared she needed good food and a great deal of rest. "You poor lass, life's not been easy, lately, has it?" she said gently; and plunged off into lively chatter before Elizabeth could feel the need to answer.

Elizabeth promised herself she would give the peace of Oak Bend a week to loosen the knots in her nerves before she let herself begin thinking. And it was only after a couple of days, when her own tension began to ease a little, that she noticed that something of the old spontaneity of Molly's liveliness was missing.

Once or twice her thoughts seemed far away, and

Elizabeth saw her look at Jim with troubled eyes.

One morning when they were alone together Elizabeth said carefully, "Molly, is Jim ill?"

"Ill? Gracious no." She looked at Elizabeth sharply. "Or not that I know of." Her forehead creased anxiously. "What makes you ask that? Has he said something to you about not feeling well?"

"No, no." Elizabeth shook her head. "Nothing like that. It's just that I've seen you watching him as if you were worried about him. Three times this morning you've gone outside to look down to where he has the horse-team, ploughing. I'm not trying to pry. I just wondered if he were ill, that's all."

"Do I make it so obvious?" Molly made a rueful face. "I try not to. Jim laughs at me and says I'm fussing over nothing. You see, it's the aborigines."

"Surely you haven't had another visit from the group who gave us that awful fright when I was here before?"

"No. By the way, we heard afterwards they had been out on a pay-back expedition because one of the local tribe, the Kabi, had killed a member of their tribe. They were heading home again. No, this is different."

She paused. "Jim was ploughing up some new land and he found some piles of stone in the way, so he moved them and ploughed the ground. It seems they've been sacred to the aborigines for goodness knows how long – centuries, maybe thousands of years – and they had some very special meaning. Jim didn't know, of course – he's very careful about not breaking any aboriginal laws. It seems the elders of the tribe were frightfully angry and made some kind of vow that misfortune would come on us.

"Jim put the stones back as soon as he found out they were special, and stopped ploughing in the area. Birindjie, who is the headman's son, works for Jim sometimes on the farm, along with one or two of the other natives, and he came to Jim and told him what he'd done. He said it was 'bad feller' thing, and told us about the curse, or whatever it is."

"Black magic?" Elizabeth smiled.

Molly shook her head. "It's no use to joke about it. I don't think I set much store by a curse, if that's what they've put on us. Or perhaps it's not that *they* put the curse on us for touching the stones. It's the spirit-people who became the stones, as far as I can gather, who might have their vengeance on us. Oh, all right, I know it makes no sense to us. But I've seen more of these people than you have, my dear. They have ways we don't even begin to understand."

"But Molly!" Elizabeth was still smiling. "You must half believe they have some sort of magic powers, or you wouldn't be so concerned. Now come on. You don't *really* believe in any such thing, do you?"

Molly hesitated, and said slowly, "They're camped, at the moment, just around that far bend of the river. I don't know about the magic. I think what hangs in the back of my mind is something a trifle more concrete."

Elizabeth looked at her sharply. "I thought Jim and the local tribe got on well? Surely you don't think the natives would harm him!"

"I don't *think* so, but I don't know. That's just it, you see: we don't understand enough about their laws. There's this pay-back thing which decrees that if one person is killed, a life has to be taken in retaliation. If you can't get the killer, a member of his family will do. Or a member of his tribe, if the victim was of another tribe. I don't know whether that law extends to destruction of sacred totems."

It was next morning at breakfast in the big kitchen which

the wood-burning iron stove made almost too warm, that Jim asked Molly to put up some lunch for him.

"I want to do some fencing in the bottom river-paddock, so if you'll put up some bread and a bit of cheese and some tea and sugar, I'll boil the billy on the job."

"Birindjie and Ngarana going with you?" Molly asked, carefully casual.

"No. I haven't seen them for a few days. Maybe they've gone walkabout."

Molly sighed. "I wish you could get some regular labour to help, Jim. You can't depend on the blacks."

He smiled. "That's their nature, lass. They've lived for thousands of years, those people, without regular working hours. Can't expect them to change, not in this generation nor the next. Why should they? It's only curiosity that makes them work for me at all. It's not need. They've had all they needed since the dreamtime without worrying about stuff like the whites' money, or their rations."

"I know all that, but you still need help. I'm sorry, but I'm not very good at cooking witchetty grubs or goanna over the coals. We do live European lives, and I imagine we're not about to change, either. So, to run this place you must have labour."

Jim nodded. "I surely do need a couple of men, like I had before the gold took them all. But soon I'll be able to get men to come back to the land to work. The gold's running out, except for the deep reef stuff. Meanwhile," he added, getting to his feet, "I'd better get on with the work."

The day passed pleasantly, and Elizabeth felt Molly seemed more relaxed. But perhaps that was because she herself was beginning to feel a little less tense and desperate.

She helped Molly make a batch of fresh bread, and then

went out into the garden to weed among the vegetables and take a long, luxuriant breath of rose-perfume in the flower garden, trying not to wonder how long it was since she had smelt a rose.

Sarah, watching her, came over. "Can I smell it, too?"

She sniffed deeply. "Mmm. That's pretty." She looked at the deep red bloom. "What is it?"

A little stab of shock caught painfully in Elizabeth's throat.

"It's a rose, sweetheart," she said.

Dear heaven, she thought, as memories swamped her: of her own childhood of spring flowers, and deep chairs before a glowing fire in winter; sleigh rides in the snow, and pretty white voile summer dresses with satin sashes; walls lined with shelves of books, and rugs on a polished floor. Oh, God, and my daughter doesn't even know what a rose is. She must have seen roses in Sydney, but this accursed goldfield has swamped them from her memory. All she knows is dreariness and mud.

John's voice came clearly in her mind: "I can give you the kind of life you should have – you and Sarah."

She shut her eyes. I promised myself I wouldn't think about that – not yet, she told herself; how can I ever think of such a thing, anyway? I, leave my husband for another man?

It's because you think he's a murderer. That's the truth, isn't it?

John's voice again. And saying more. Saying: I love you. Remember, you can trust me. Always.

Sarah's voice broke in. "Do you remember, when we were here last time at Aunt Molly's, some black men came? And Edward and I had to hide behind a curtain? I was real scared. But Edward was as brave as anything. Wasn't he?"

Elizabeth nodded. "Yes," she said, trying to keep her

voice steady. "As brave as anything."

Sarah ran off to play at throwing a stick for Sandy the dog to chase and bring back, and Elizabeth turned away and suddenly began to cry, great shaking sobs of anguish.

Molly went quickly to her and put her arms around her, saying nothing, but just holding her.

Presently Elizabeth raised her head. "I'm sorry," she said shakily.

Molly smiled. "Don't be. You haven't done enough crying since Edward died, and that's the truth, isn't it? Bottling it all up inside you till you look like a ghost walking, so pale and thin."

Since Edward died. Elizabeth thought incredulously: it's only a few weeks, really; a few weeks, and all my world has fallen in pieces.

As if Edward's death hadn't been enough, there was everything that followed it. Dr Miller's death, and the fear, the dreadful fear that lay like a lump of unrelenting ice in her stomach.

She wondered if Robert knew of that fear. He must, she thought. Then if he were innocent, why didn't he tell her so? Never once had he said he hadn't killed Abraham Miller. Why hadn't she asked? Because it was an admission of doubt? Or because she could not believe him?

"What's left between people when trust is gone?" John Trent had asked.

John, the quiet, loyal, dependable one.

What would life with John be like? Never like life with Robert – a wild mixture of gaiety and passion and despair. John –

She turned and looked at the weatherboard house with its wide verandahs and its look of solid prosperity. This was what John could give her: the security she longed for and would never have with Robert.

Sarah would not have to ask what a rose was.

Elizabeth pulled herself back to her surroundings, aware that Molly had asked her something.

"I'm sorry," she said. "I was wool-gathering. What did you say?"

"Only that I thought it might be a good idea if you went and lay down for a bit. You look so weary."

Elizabeth smiled faintly and shook her head. "I'm all right now, Molly. You're a dear, and I'm a most unsatisfactory guest. But I feel well enough, and I'd like to work here in the garden, if you don't mind."

"Mind? Who ever minded someone else pulling weeds for them?" Molly retorted cheerfully. "But don't go making yourself overtired and ill."

"I shan't. And I want to be tired enough to sleep. Too much thinking in the dark isn't good."

She very deliberately kept herself busy for the rest of the day. She didn't want to do any thinking at all at the moment.

But as the day wore on, she gradually became conscious of Molly's mounting restlessness. By sunset she was almost constantly watching from the kitchen window the slope down to the river. She chatted cheerfully and made no mention of her concern for Jim but, with the evening meal almost ready, her uneasiness increased.

She lit the oil lamp that hung from the ceiling, and its light flung reflections on the window-glass which prevented them from seeing out.

"Jim's late," she said finally.

"Well, it must be a longish ride to the paddock where he was going to work," Elizabeth suggested.

"Oh, yes, close on a mile." She bunched up her calico apron to protect her hand while she gripped the knob of the oven door and opened it to check the dinner roasting inside. "And he may have worked till he couldn't see any longer," she added. "So of course he won't get home till late."

They waited.

Conversation became strained and desultory as they both found themselves listening for hoofbeats.

No hoofbeats came, and the time dragged on till it reached the point where they both knew, though neither spoke the thought, that Jim had had more than enough time to ride a mile, even in the dark.

Molly went several times to the door and looked down to the river where the small points of firelight that marked where the aborigines were camped a quarter-mile or more away, winked through the trees that hid the camp from view from the house by day.

They gave Sarah her dinner and put her to bed, unaware of their concern.

"Dinner will spoil," Molly said eventually. "We'd better have ours. Serves the man right if his meal is ruined, making us wait like this," she added with one last effort to be lighthearted.

They found they had no appetite. A strong north-west wind had got up, somehow only adding to their sense of foreboding as it blotted out all other sound.

Around ten o'clock Molly said quietly, "We may as well go to bed, Elizabeth. He's not coming home tonight."

She managed a wry smile. "And try to get some sleep, my dear. Here we were, thinking to get you away from your own troubles for a while, and now you're landed with ours. But let's not be thinking the worst," she added firmly. "It's happened before that he was out on a job that took longer than he planned, and sooner than ride home in the dark, he's just camped where he was till daylight. It's not a good idea to ride through the bush at night, where a low-hanging branch you don't see can knock a rider out. There's nothing we can do till morning."

She stopped a moment, and then whispered, "Except pray."

She turned away quickly. "I'll just get the bedroom candles before I put this lamp out."

Elizabeth lay awake in the darkness, knowing Molly would be sleepless also.

Around midnight the blustering wind began to decrease, and presently dropped to stillness. Elizabeth got up and went to the window.

The stars were brilliant, but she could no longer see the camp-fires by the river. The fires would not be out, because on pain of getting a thumping from their men in the morning the women would have to keep rousing from sleep to tend the remnants of the fires to keep a few tiny embers alive, ready to be fanned to fresh flame when needed. The men could relight the fires by rubbing two sticks together till they heated to combustion level, but it was tedious, detested work.

Presently Elizabeth became aware of a faint, high-pitched sound and she pushed up the sash window to listen.

Somewhere off in the distance a dingo pack was howling and intermittently yelping. It was the long rise and fall of the howling which, she had always felt on the few occasions she had heard it, must be one of the loneliest sounds on earth.

The dingoes probably had a cow and calf at bay, though she could hear no bellowing of cattle in rage and terror. She shivered at the primitive savagery of the sound. The pack would have selected a calf and cut it and its mother out of the herd, and now they would circle and feint and snap, dodging the raking horns of the cow as she tried to defend her calf, waiting their chance till they could separate the two, and bring the calf down.

Elizabeth had never seen the tawny wild dogs hunting, but Jim Burton had described their tactics. Normally, they would hunt native game but, particularly in a winter shortage of their normal prey, they would sometimes turn to attacking cattle.

Elizabeth closed the window again, as much against the sound of the dingoes as against the chill of the night air.

Jim would be all right, she tried to tell herself. He was a highly competent and experienced bushman and, as Molly had said, it would not be the first time he'd been overtaken by darkness away from home and chosen to camp rather than risk an accident.

She didn't believe in any curse falling on Jim because he had moved some sacred stones accidentally. And surely the aborigines wouldn't harm a man who had befriended them, simply because he unwittingly broke one of their laws.

And yet, as Molly had said, how important was that law? How could a European know if it invoked a death-penalty?

She slept a little, fitfully, waiting anxiously for dawn. As the first greyness of approaching day invaded the room she got up quietly and dressed. Sarah was still soundly and peacefully asleep as she slipped out into the hall, almost bumping into Molly emerging from her room.

"I'll light the fire and get a bit of warmth in the kitchen," Molly said. "A cup of tea will help us start the day, and by then it'll be light enough to see."

It did not need to get any lighter. While Molly laid kindling in the firebox of the kitchen stove, Elizabeth went to the door and looked out.

"Molly!" she cried sharply. "Look!"

Jim's horse, still wearing bridle and saddle, was idly cropping grass down near the stables.

"Oh, God," Molly whispered. Then she squared her shoulders. "We must get help as fast as we can. Someone had better go to Gympie and fetch a doctor. It's a hundred to one he'll be needed, and we can't waste time waiting till we find Jim before someone sets out. We must start looking at once. And we must get the neighbours – we may need them for a search-party. And –"

"Molly," Elizabeth cut in quietly, "there's no one to send on errands."

Molly was tying on a riding-bonnet. "We must get the aborigines," she said practically.

"But I thought you were afraid they'd harmed Jim!"

The thing that had festered in their minds since sunset yesterday had been spoken at last.

Molly looked at her, her eyes dark with desperation. "They may have," she said levelly. "And they may not. I haven't any choice but to trust them. They're the only help we have. The nearest neighbours – the Rices – are three miles away across country. I'm going for the aborigines."

Elizabeth nodded. "I'll come with you."

"Can you ride?"

Elizabeth smiled. "I can ride."

She woke Sarah, gave her a glass of milk and some bread and butter, and told her what was happening. "Will you stay here in the house all by yourself till Aunt Molly and I come back?"

Sarah nodded solemnly. "Will you tell Daddy when we go home that I was as brave as anything?"

"Yes, of course. As brave as anything."

"Mummy." Sarah's voice stopped her at the door. "Uncle Jim hasn't got dead like Edward, has he?"

Elizabeth hesitated. "We don't think so, sweetheart."

Don't we? she wondered as she hurried out. She checked her step, aware suddenly of how devastatingly alone Sarah would feel, all alone while her mother and Molly rode off on some only-half-understood mission. She called Sandy, Sarah's dog. "Sandy can stay in the house with you, sweetheart," she said, while Sandy, delighted at this licence, looked as pleased as Sarah.

Molly, already mounted astride Jim's horse to save precious time changing its saddle for a lady's side-saddle, was holding Elizabeth's horse. She watched her swing into the saddle.

"And to think I asked if you could ride," she said.

"I doubt if my cavalryman-husband would ever have married me if I couldn't," Elizabeth smiled. "Lead off. I'll be right behind you."

They rode at a gallop around the river to the aborigines' camp, where people were already stirring. The women reined in their horses as the black people's dogs came rushing out with a great barking. A tall young man wearing a pair of tattered trousers came forward.

"Missus!" he said sharply.

Elizabeth felt herself tense. If these people had harmed – She stopped her own thought-words. It was time to face the truth. If these people had killed Jim, how would they react now? Until that moment she had never even wondered about their own safety.

"Birindjie!" Molly was obviously relieved to see him, and Elizabeth remembered that was the name of one of the men who worked sometimes for Jim.

"Boss lost," Molly was saying urgently. "Go that way yesterday." She pointed north-west along the river. "Make fence in bottom paddock. Not come back. Horse come." She patted the neck of the gelding she rode. "Saddle, bridle. Not boss."

Birindjie wheeled around and spoke rapidly in their own tongue to the crowd of curious onlookers who had gathered.

"We come, missus," he said.

"Birindjie, will you take a horse from the stockyard, ride Gympie town, get doctor? You understand doctor?"

He didn't even answer, but set off at a run for the stockyards.

Molly looked around. "Ngarana? Oh, there you are. Will you take horse, go tell Mr Rice boss lost?"

The bearded young man trotted off after Birindjie.

An older man with grizzled hair said, "Missus, we find."

Half a dozen men gathered around and looked at the hoofs of the horse Jim had ridden, then, watching the ground, they set off for the homestead at the tireless lope they could keep up for hours.

"Come," Molly said to Elizabeth, and they set their horses at a trot behind the men.

Near the stables the aborigines halted and began to cast about in widening circles, intently eyeing the ground.

"What are they doing?" Elizabeth asked.

"Trying to pick up the tracks the horse made as he came home last night," Molly said.

One man called to the others and pointed at the ground, and then pointed off in a south-westerly direction, and they all set off, watching the ground, moving with increasing confidence as the one track apparently sorted itself out from others made by other horses.

"No, no!" Molly called. "Not that way! They're going the wrong way," she added to Elizabeth. "That's almost the opposite direction to the way Jim went."

She called again, riding after them, "No! That way!" She pointed north. "Boss go that way!"

The men stopped and looked at Molly. The older man who had first offered to do the tracking shook his head and pointed at the ground, and then again in a south-westerly direction.

"Horse come," he said.

"Not this horse," Molly objected. "Not last night."

"Horse come," he insisted, and the group of men set off again, speaking occasionally among themselves, pointing at some sign they saw on the ground.

The women rode behind the trackers, unable to see a trace of the trail the men followed at a trot.

If there was a trail to see, Elizabeth thought bitterly. Was this whole exercise an elaborate hoax to try to cover up murder, or at least to try to allay suspicion of their involvement? While these men led her and Molly off in a wrong direction, were other members of the tribe disposing of evidence, knowing their law and the white man's law often clashed head-on? She wondered whether Molly's thoughts were running a similar course as, pale and silent, she rode with her gaze on the muscular black bodies that trotted steadily ahead.

Elizabeth urged her horse up beside Molly's. "Can you see any hoof-marks?" she asked.

Molly shook her head. "Nothing. And how would I know which horse made them, or when? Oh, I know," she added, her face drawn and set. "I know what you're thinking: maybe there is no trail, and we're being led a wild goose chase. But the fact we can see nothing doesn't mean there's nothing to see. These people for hundreds of generations have learned the meaning of a tiny bit of scuffed earth, or a newly-snapped twig, or a bruised blade of grass."

"But they seem so sure!"

"Oh, they do that. And this is never the way to the river-paddock. But we've got to follow. We've no choice but to trust them."

What's left between people when trust is gone?

Elizabeth shut her eyes for a moment. I will not let myself begin thinking of that now, she told herself firmly.

Still the dark men led, ignoring the white women, intent and purposeful. They went in a long sweep around the river, only once or twice even hesitating as if they had lost the trail, then picking it up with a pointing finger or a guttural exclamation and moving on swiftly.

They had gone perhaps half a mile, perhaps more, when one of the men gave a shout and, looking back at Molly, pointed ahead.

"Jim!" Molly cried, and kicked her horse to a gallop.

A couple of hundred yards away a man sat slumped against the trunk of a gum-tree. Elizabeth felt a wave of swamping relief as he raised his head at the sound of hoofbeats. Then Molly was swinging down from the saddle to kneel beside him, her arms around him, holding him wordlessly.

When Elizabeth drew up he was smiling crookedly and saying, "Now, lass, I'm all right. It's over now and I'm all right."

He was pale and haggard and his eyes were dark with pain and stress. His left trouser-leg was ripped and saturated with blood, stiff where it was partly dried.

The two women carefully eased the torn cloth away from the wound – an ugly four-inch slash on the inside of the leg below the knee, blood still seeping from it. Hitching up her skirt, Molly slipped off a white cotton petticoat and they tore it into strips and carefully padded and bound the wound.

"But what happened, Jim? What are you doing *here*?" Molly asked as she worked, pausing now and then to look at him as if to reassure herself he was alive. "You said you were going to the bottom paddock, and I wanted the men to go there, but they wouldn't because they said the horse had come this way. What happened?"

"I finished early at the job I was doing in the river-paddock, so I thought I'd check the cattle in the south boundary paddock. It would mean I'd more or less ride a triangle by the time I got home. That's why the horse went home from what looked like the wrong direction."

"But the leg!" Molly said. "However did you come to cut yourself so?"

"Well, you know I like to keep the south boundary fence in one piece, whatever happens to the others."

He looked at Elizabeth with a wry face. "The neighbours on that side don't like wandering cattle. Anyway, I found a bit of fence down, and I went to cut a sapling for repairs. But the axe glanced off and gashed my leg. I managed to tear a bit off my shirt and bind it a bit, but I couldn't stop the bleeding."

"You should never be this far from the house on your own," Molly said worriedly.

"Now, lass," he reasoned, touching her hair with his hand, "if a man acted like that in this country, how would he get on?"

She sighed. "I know, I know. Was the leg so bad you couldn't get on the horse?"

"I tried." He looked embarrassed. "Such a fool thing: when I tried to get in the saddle, I fainted."

"Small wonder, with a leg like that. I'll not have you call my husband a fool," Molly said sternly.

He smiled at her. "It was getting dusk, and I must have been out for a bit – I think I must have hit my head as well when I fell. Anyway, it was almost dark when I came to."

A look of near-horror stared in his eyes as he remembered.

"There were dingoes," he said. "I didn't believe it for a moment. I thought I was dreaming. But they were real, all right. Half a dozen or more, all around me. They were excited by the blood and they were sniffing my leg and

growling and snapping at each other. Until I moved, they
no doubt thought I was dead. When I sat up they backed
off, but only a few yards.''

Elizabeth shuddered. ''I heard them! Jim, in the middle
of the night I heard them – howling and yelping as if they
had something at bay. I thought of a cow and calf. I never
dreamed –''

''Of course not. And what could you have done,
anyway?''

Remembering the savagery of the sound of the pack,
Elizabeth said, ''What did you do?''

''Almost died of fright on the spot,'' Jim said ruefully.
''The horse had gone – who could blame him? – and I'd put
the axe back in its sheath on the saddle, so I hadn't a thing
to defend myself with, and I couldn't walk.

''I've heard,'' he added, ''that dingoes have never been
known to attack a live human being, but I found I had no
desire to set a precedent. They jumped back a bit whenever
I moved, but they didn't go far, and they kept circling back.
The tree had a couple of low branches, fortunately, so
eventually I managed to haul myself up on to one a few feet
off the ground. I wager that if that pack had been around at
the time I'd have made it into the saddle in the first place.
Those dingoes spent all night within about a hundred yards
of the tree, howling and sometimes fighting among
themselves. Sometimes they came close enough for me to
see them slinking around, as if they were waiting for me to
die and fall down. I still felt queasy, so I fastened myself to
the tree with my belt so I wouldn't fall if I did pass out
again.''

''Jim!'' Molly didn't seem able to say any more.

''I've had pleasanter nightmares,'' he admitted. ''I tried
cooeeing for help, but the wind snatched the sound away.''

Elizabeth rode back to the homestead to reassure Sarah and wait for the doctor and the neighbours to come, while the aborigines carefully and slowly carried Jim, and Molly walked beside him.

With the fear lifted, Elizabeth exulted in the ride back to the house, putting the horse to the gallop up the long gentle slopes, thrilling to the wind in her hair. How long was it since she had had the chance to ride a good horse?

How long would it be again?

Ten

Jim's leg needed a number of stitches and the doctor ordered him to bed for a week. When Jim protested the doctor, snapping his medical bag shut, shrugged.

"Be thankful you're still alive. You gave your head a nasty crack when you fell trying to get on your horse, and you lost a lot of blood."

When the doctor had gone Elizabeth, sitting with Jim while Molly prepared him a meal, said wonderingly, "Those native men bewildered me. I've heard stories of how wonderful they are at tracking, but – Jim, they followed your horse's trail at a trot, and they knew it was that horse, not any other, and they knew the track was fresh, no older than yesterday. And only once, in a patch of sand by the river where he'd gone down to drink, could I see any kind of tracks – and then those hoofmarks could have been made by any horse on the station, for all I knew. But they knew. I didn't believe it, but they *knew!*"

He nodded. "They learn from earliest childhood and they never stop studying, and their skill seems uncanny to us, but to them it's simple logic."

Elizabeth said slowly, "I've heard people refer to the aborigines as ignorant savages. I'm supposed to be an educated woman, but I know who was the ignorant one out there this morning."

Jim smiled. "Ah, yes, I know. But ignorance is just a matter of surroundings and a particular way of life. As you say, we are as ignorant when confronted with their lifestyle as they are when confronted with ours."

He looked absent for a moment, and a shade of sadness brushed across his face.

"We will destroy them, you know. Mostly it won't be deliberate and it won't be due to malice. But we will destroy them, simply because we have brought another kind of life that will seize them like a disease. Sometimes –"

He moved his hands restlessly as if he searched for words to clarify his thoughts.

"Sometimes I wonder if we will destroy ourselves, in the end. Because we're not like these dark people. They'd never destroy themselves because they're a part of nature, while we're alien – not just alien to this country, but almost alien to the earth itself. We live *on* the land, but the aborigines live *with* it."

He looked up at her and smiled almost in embarrassment. "What nonsense I do go on with! I must have hit my head harder than I thought. What do you suppose that wife of mine is cooking? No delicate invalid's meal, I hope – I'm famished."

When Jim was on his feet again, Elizabeth and Sarah went back to Gympie, and Robert.

Birindjie drove them in the Burtons' buggy. "You'll be safe with Birindjie," they had assured her, and the handsome young black man had clearly thoroughly enjoyed the importance of being allowed to drive the buggy and pair, and had surprised Elizabeth with his skill with the horses. She was beginning to understand the Burtons' respect for the aborigines and their affection for Birindjie in particular.

Elizabeth's arrival back in town in a buggy driven by an aborigine drew some attention. Robert had just stepped out of Trent's General Store as Birindjie drove up the street and he looked up, surprise in his face, and stepped out and signalled Birindjie to stop.

"If I'd known you were ready to come home I'd have borrowed a horse and trap from somewhere and come out for you," he told Elizabeth.

She looked at him, searching his face as if she could find there the answer she could only find in herself.

"Hello, Robert." He was thinner, and tense-looking, as if the strain were taking toll of his strength in spite of himself. "There was no need to trouble you. Birindjie managed beautifully."

The young man grinned with a flash of white teeth.

"Thank you for bringing my family home, Birindjie." Robert nodded to him. "The ground on the way to our place is very rough – hardly fit for a buggy. I'll help the ladies down here and carry their baggage home, so you can get back to Oak Bend before dark."

Sarah was almost bursting with impatience. "Daddy, Daddy! You haven't said hello. And Sandy's here, too."

Sandy, tongue lolling, tail waving madly, was half hanging over the side of the buggy with excitement.

Robert laughed and held up his arms to his daughter. "Welcome home, Princess. Jump!" He caught her and hugged her and set her down while Sandy leapt down beside her.

Then he reached up a hand to help Elizabeth down. As she stepped down he pulled her almost roughly against him and held her in a long fierce kiss which she felt oddly stemmed not so much from his hunger for her as from his desire to say to the onlookers: this woman is mine; take note of it.

She drew away from him with a little laugh. "Robert! People are staring."

"Good." He laughed down at her, but there was no gaiety in his eyes. "We *are* married."

That night, she felt his love-making had the same quality – not of need but of possessiveness. He wanted to demonstrate to her, as he had wanted to demonstrate to the town, that she was his.

He can't know about John, she thought; he can't. And surely I've never let him guess I think he killed Dr Miller. And yet there is no way, I suppose, that I have ever been able to really hide the fact that I find no joy in him any longer. And when he does know about John, when I tell him, what will he do, Robert the unpredictable?

He would let her go, almost without a word.

Strange that she should be so sure of that, she reflected. But there would be no scenes, no recriminations. Robert was a good loser; always had been. He'd had plenty of practice, she thought bitterly.

Suddenly she realised that her mind had said: "When he does know about John, when I tell him –" When, not if. Had she, then, already made her decision?

She turned her face to the wall and wept silently in the darkness.

She didn't sleep till nearly morning, and even then she seemed to be only lightly dozing when Sarah burst in.

"Mummy! Daddy!" Her voice was puzzled and half-fearful. "Where did this funny thing come from?"

Elizabeth sat up swiftly. "What thing, Sarah?"

The sun was just thrusting brilliantly over the hills into a wind-polished sky, and she could see that Sarah, already dressed, held nothing in her hands.

"What thing, darling?" she asked again.

"This thing outside – a kind of post."

Robert, tousled and half-asleep, pushed himself up, reaching for his trousers, seeming filled with the same sense of alarm that gripped Elizabeth as she flung a shawl over her nightgown. They reached the door together.

"There," Sarah said. "Where did it come from?"

A post had been pushed stealthily into the soft earth that heaped near the shaft of Robert's mine: a post with an arm at the top, and a dangling hangman's noose.

Sick, Elizabeth turned her head away and leaned against the doorpost.

Robert strode out without a word and pushed the gallows over. He took an axe and chopped the rope through in several places and flung the pieces down the shaft.

"What is it?" Sarah demanded.

"Someone's idea of a joke," Elizabeth told her, fighting to keep her voice steady.

"I don't like it," Sarah said, backing away from the pieces of timber.

"Never mind, darling," Elizabeth said. "Whatever it was before, it's just a bit of old rubbish now. Daddy can chop it up and we'll use it for firewood, so really whoever put it there has done us a good turn," she added with an attempt at cheerfulness.

Then she added, "How did you come to wake up and find it? Did you hear someone outside?"

"No," Sarah said, reminded. "I heard Sandy making a funny noise and I got up to talk to him. Where is he?"

Sandy usually slept beside Sarah's bed because, although dogs were not perhaps as highly prized as cats for keeping down the hordes of rats and mice, Sandy was a good ratter and might well be stolen.

But Sandy was not in his usual spot. He was lying prone against the wall beside the hearth and when Sarah called him he tried to sit up, gave a strange half-choking moan and slumped down again, his legs slipping from under him at odd angles, unable to support him.

"Daddy!" Sarah screamed.

Robert was in the doorway in an instant, axe in hand.

"Sandy's sick!" Sarah cried, pointing.

Robert dropped the axe and came forward to where Elizabeth knelt beside the dog.

"They've poisoned him!" he said. "The bastards have poisoned him."

"But Robert, he was in the house," Elizabeth objected. "No one could have got to him last night."

"They might have done it yesterday afternoon. Left a bit of meat lying around, full of strychnine or arsenic. Poisons don't always act at once. And it mightn't have been a very big dose."

"Why?" Sarah sobbed, crouching down and putting her face in Sandy's smooth black and tan coat. "Why would they poison Sandy?"

No one answered her. Elizabeth looked wordlessly at Robert, and he understood the unspoken question.

"We'll leave him for a while. If he gets too bad I'll put an end to it."

Elizabeth put a blanket over him. Most of the time he lay quietly, and even when he began struggling convulsively it seemed more out of fear and anger at his own helplessness than out of pain.

"Can we get Uncle John to come?" Sarah asked once. "He might know what to do."

"I don't think so, sweetheart," Elizabeth said.

It was Bert Peters who came by a couple of hours later.

"Hello," he said cheerfully at the doorway. "Everyone's looking very glum this morning. Trouble?"

"Sandy's sick," Sarah told him.

His eyes went to the blanket-covered form on the floor and he crossed the room in a few strides without waiting to be asked in.

"Damn," he said. "Damn and damn and damn! Why didn't I think of it?"

"Think of what?" Robert asked.

Bert, his face intent, was running his hands carefully over the dog's head and neck, his fingers combing through the short, thick hair.

In a moment he gave a little grunt, parted the hair in one spot on the side of Sandy's neck and made a little pulling movement.

"That," he said, holding out his hand.

In his palm was a tiny blue-grey creature which looked rather like a short-legged spider not half the size of a woman's little finger nail. "I should have warned you to keep searching him for these."

"What is it?" Elizabeth asked, puzzled.

"Scrub tick," Bert answered tersely, dropping it into the fire. "Come, old boy, let's make sure you don't have any more." He began feeling through Sandy's hair again.

Elizabeth said, "Do you mean to tell us that *that* tiny thing has done this to Sandy?"

Bert nodded. "One is enough, if it's been stuck in his skin a few days. They're parasites – blood-suckers – and they attach themselves to an animal and even though there must be a very tiny bit of poison in their bite, it's enough to paralyse a dog or a cat. I just want to check he don't have no more."

"Will he be all right?" Sarah demanded anxiously.

Bert hesitated, looking at the little girl. "Well, we're sure going to try to get him well again," he said cautiously. "Tell you what, suppose I take him over to my place to look after till he's well again? We'll wrap him in this blanket and your Daddy will help me carry him so we don't hurt him. All right?"

"I want to be with him!" Sarah said, and began to cry.

Elizabeth held her, trying to console her, while the men went out, carefully carrying the paralysed dog.

"Is he going to die?" Robert asked Bert when they got outside.

"Well, he's more likely to die than live. The poison doesn't seem to stop working for about a day after you get the tick out, and the animal goes on getting worse. I don't know how much worse Sandy can get, and still live. But it ain't a nice thing to watch, live or die. Better Sarah doesn't have to see."

"Maybe we should put him out of his misery," Robert suggested. "I don't like to see an animal suffering for nothing."

Bert shook his head. "I'd say he's got a chance of living. Not much, but some. And I don't think he's really in pain, or not much pain. It just looks that way, I think."

When Robert went back to the shack Elizabeth met him outside. "Is he dying?" she asked in a low voice.

Robert shrugged, not looking at her. "Bert doesn't know. Probably, yes, but maybe not."

"What can he do for him?"

"Nothing except keep turning him over every couple of hours to try to stop him getting pneumonia. That, and keep him where Sarah can't see him."

"How much more does Sarah have to suffer in this place?" Elizabeth asked bitterly, but her question was directed as much at life itself as at Robert.

She looked at him after a moment. "Robert, that gallows –" She shivered. "It's ugly, and even dangerous, perhaps. If someone hates – us, as much as that, it could be dangerous. Suppose –"

She stopped, her face contorting slightly in horror as a thought struck her.

She shook her head. "No. It's too horrible. I don't want to think it."

"Suppose what?" he demanded, his voice rough.

"Oh, it's just my imagination running riot. But – well, Dr Miller's house was burned. Suppose whoever was sick enough to erect a gallows outside our door should set fire to the shack one night?"

He looked at her long and hard. Then he picked up a handful of little stones and began tossing them idly one by one toward the mine-shaft.

"I didn't tell you last night, but there's a rumour of a new gold-strike in Victoria. If it seems to have anything in it, I thought we might move on down there."

Move on.

She walked away a few paces. Move on. How many times had she heard those words? Yet never had they carried quite the impact they had now.

Deaf to Robert's eager words telling of the stories he had heard of the new Victorian strike, she looked along the river and up over the hills. The town looked no less crude now than it had all those months ago when they had arrived. The slab and bark huts, some of them empty now – mute testimony to empty dreams; the raw, trampled earth looking as if it had been blasted by a fearful cannon-barrage; the tents; the lines of flapping washing where women tried to make a home.

She would leave this, as John had pointed out, for other diggings just as dreary, just as full of futile hopes; or for some other dream of Robert's just as uncertain.

Move on.

Those words now brought her headlong into making her decision: Robert and this kind of life, probably forever, because she was bound to him by a contract called marriage; or John, and security for herself and Sarah.

Strange, she reflected: the idea of leaving her husband for another man, unthinkable in her English drawing-room, had a different aspect in these rough surroundings. Here there were many things unthinkable in her English drawing-room. She had heard of many a miner down on his luck who had come up from his shaft one day, or home from the hotel one night, to find his wife had left with another digger who had seen his pick uncover the dull gleam of gold.

Am I no better than that? she wondered.

But she knew, as John Trent knew, that if Abraham Miller had not died, she would never have left Robert.

This country was not England, and what was unthinkable there could be an exercise in survival here.

In what English drawing-room would you hear a neighbour tell of how her husband, having come to the diggings and built a shack, had sent for her and their children to come from Brisbane by coastal trader some eighty miles to a tiny river-mouth trading-port called Maroochydore from the aboriginal word for the black swan, then by smaller boat some miles up the river to where a horse and cart were waiting to take them the last fifty miles over crude tracks. But the cart was smashed and they had to set out, with three days' food, to walk – a walk that became a three weeks' nightmare, with the track lost, having to cut their way through the bush.

This was not England.

Robert had always insisted before that he wouldn't leave because leaving was tantamount to admitting guilt. And he had never said, "I am not guilty." He had said instead, "Let them think what they like. They can't prove anything. They can't touch me."

Now he was talking of leaving. Was it even now an an admission of guilt?

"What do you think?" Robert asked at her elbow.

She started, wondering for a moment if she had spoken her thoughts aloud.

"I beg your pardon?"

He was looking at her strangely. "What do you think about going to Victoria?"

"I – I don't know." She tried to gather her thoughts. "When – would you think of leaving?"

"When I hear a bit more about it – see if there's anything in it. Quite a few fellows have gone already." He paused and frowned. "I'd have thought you'd have been anxious to go – anywhere away from here."

She turned to him, a terrible question in her eyes. But it was not that question she asked.

"Robert, why must it always be another goldfield, another dream with little chance of coming true?"

If he understood the question in her eyes, he chose to answer only the spoken one.

He gave a little laugh. "Oh, come on, Liz! Where's your sense of adventure, my Elizabeth?"

"Dead," she answered. "Like too many people."

She turned away from him and went into the shack.

All through the day, Bert Peters told them grimly, Sandy grew worse, till by nightfall all he could do was gently thump his tail when spoken to. The rest of his body was totally paralysed, his breathing was a strange moaning sound, and his eyes were glazed like those of a dead animal.

Robert said, "Let me shoot him."

But Bert, after a moment's hesitation, shook his head. "He still might make it. It's a queer thing. You can't never be sure. They can be real bad, and live; they can look as if it's only a mild case, and die. You can't never be sure."

Sandy was still alive next morning, neither better nor worse, Bert reported, and firmly but cheerfully put aside Sarah's pleas to be allowed to see him.

"You see," he told her, "Sandy's very weak. If he sees you, he'll get real excited because he loves you, and that might be bad for him."

Sarah reluctantly accepted the argument. Elizabeth did everything she could to fill Sarah's hours with lessons and games – pushing her own tormenting thoughts away, to be considered only in long night hours of sleeplessness. Robert took Sarah for a walk, and made urgent surreptitious enquiries around the town for a puppy, should Sandy die; but puppies were scarce.

John Trent came and took Sarah to ride on his German waggon while he delivered goods around the town.

When he could, he made an opportunity to speak alone with Elizabeth.

"I heard about the gallows," he said quietly, his eyes distressed. "Please, my dear Elizabeth, you can't go on like this."

"No," she said flatly. "Perhaps even Robert sees that. He's talking of moving down to Victoria to this new gold strike there's talk of. I don't know if it's just the lure of the gold or whether he sees this as a chance to leave here without seeming to run away."

"Leave!" John stared at her. "When?"

Elizabeth shook her head. "He says when he sees whether there seems to be any weight in the rumours about the new field."

"I see." John was silent a moment. "Well, the rumours do seem to be based on fact. They've become a bit more than rumours now." He caught her hands. "My dear, you must have thought about what I've asked you to do."

She nodded, not meeting his eyes. "Sometimes I think I'm not capable of thinking of anything else."

"And?" His grip on her hands tightened.

"I don't know. Please. Give me a little more time." She raised her head and looked at him. "I promise I'll make my decision soon – before Robert leaves, if he decides to leave."

John slowly released her hands. He stood looking at her for a long moment, half turned toward the door, then turned back and took a step toward her. He began to hold out his hands to her, and then almost with a wrenching movement he swung around on his heel and strode out.

Elizabeth turned and leaned her head against the roughly-daubed mud plaster that lined the walls. In that moment, if John had caught her in his arms, she might have found it easy to forget that she was Robert's wife.

Sandy lived for four days in total helplessness.

On the morning of the fifth day Bert pounded on the door of the shack while Elizabeth was cooking breakfast and Robert was shaving at the cracked mirror hanging on the wall above the wooden bucket which served as a bath.

"It's Sandy," Bert said when Robert opened the door. "He's going to live."

When he could stem the flood of laughter and questions from Sarah, he explained that Sandy could sit up this morning, although the paralysis was still in his hind legs. The first to be affected, the hind quarters would be the last to recover. And some of the paralysis was going from his throat and tongue. Although he still couldn't drink, he had eaten some finely-chopped meat.

"Can I see him now?" Sarah begged.

"I think so. Mind, he's still very sick and he acts very funny – he won't be able to walk properly for days and he mightn't be able to drink for a while."

"Could we drip some water down his throat?" Elizabeth asked. "He must be half crazy with thirst."

"That's a pretty sure way to kill him," Bert declared. "They can't swallow. It'd choke him, or get on his lungs. He'll hang out, especially now he's eating."

He looked at Robert. "There's another piece of news," he said. "Some Brisbane newspapers came in last night. Them stories about that southern gold strike are true enough, it seems. It's a big one."

Eleven

Robert seemed no longer concerned with the thought that leaving, especially after the gallows incident, would look like running away. He was full of impatience to be gone, even though in fact there was no real confirmation of the worth of the new strike.

"As always," Elizabeth told Maggie Doyle when she went to the "Wild Swan" to tell her they were leaving, "Robert is certain that this time he will be lucky."

They were sitting in Maggie's private room upstairs, and so it was Lady Margaret and not the rough-tongued Cockney pub-keeper who answered.

"There hasn't been much luck for any of you here, has there?"

Elizabeth shook her head. "It can hardly get worse, I suppose."

Then she added at once, "It isn't Robert's fault. He can't help being the eternal optimist."

Margaret Doyle thought wryly that it was a term only a wife accustomed to mustering her loyalties could apply to a compulsive gambler.

"That's part of Robert's charm, I suppose," Elizabeth added absently. "He's always so eager for the next adventure, so certain it will turn out well this time. The human race needs men like him, or it would be forever caught in the same rut."

She smiled "Robert will always go through life joyfully trying to catch a rainbow."

There was a little silence.

"And you?" Margaret Doyle asked softly. "Will you go with him?"

Elizabeth looked at her sharply. "What do you mean?"

Margaret shrugged. "Circumstances this time are different from other occasions when you've followed his adventuring."

Elizabeth stood up. "Do you think I would desert my husband because a townful of people suspect him – without a fragment of evidence – of murder?"

"No." Margaret shook her head. "I don't think you would desert him if the whole world suspected him of murder. But you might, if *you* suspected him. Will you have some more tea?"

Staring at her, Elizabeth shook her head. "No. Thank you." She picked up her parasol and tried to pick up her thoughts.

"We're going out to Oak Bend farm to tell the Burtons we're leaving. Robert is borrowing a horse and sulky."

Maggie Doyle stood at the window, fingers gripped whitely on the curtain, and watched for Elizabeth to step out of the hotel and on to the street. In a few moments Elizabeth moved out into view, and walked in the opposite direction from John Trent's General Store.

Maggie let the curtain drop back into place and slowly went downstairs.

It was obvious to Robert and Elizabeth as soon as they drove up to the Burtons' homestead that something was wrong.

Jim and Molly greeted them warmly, but they were

clearly tense and distressed. It was Jim who explained. "Sorry if we seem a shade gloomy. Fact is, we're pretty upset. You'll remember Birindjie, the local chief's son who drove you home last time you and Sarah were here?" he asked Elizabeth.

"Of course."

"He was killed yesterday while felling a tree for me," Jim said grimly. "It glanced off another tree and swung back and hit him."

"Oh, no!" Elizabeth cried. "Your best friend among the aborigines!"

Jim nodded. "We were really fond of Birindjie."

Robert looked from Jim to Molly and back. "Is that all?" he asked.

"Robert!" Elizabeth protested.

He shook his head. "I'm not being heartless. But most of the windows are closed, and the doors, and it's a warm summer day. Are you afraid of reprisals?"

There was a little space when no one answered, and then Molly said simply, "Yes."

Jim made a little gesture of uncertainty. "It may mean no more than their talk of disaster befalling us when I moved their sacred stones. They do have this law they call payback – or that's as near as we can get in our language – which is a kind of life-for-a-life thing. But I didn't kill Birindjie."

"Ngarana came last night under cover of darkness," Molly said, adding when Jim looked about to protest, "Jim, Robert and Elizabeth should know the truth. Ngarana often worked for Jim, too," she added.

"He risked his life to come and warn us, I'm sure, because he was clearly terrified of being found out. But he came. He said –"

She paused and swallowed. "He said Jim is marked for death under their law. It doesn't matter that it was an accident. Jim set Birindjie to fell the tree, and so Jim is responsible for his death. We have to go."

"Go?" Elizabeth was staring at her.

"Leave Oak Bend," Molly said. "At once. And –" Her voice shook. "And never come back."

"But – leave!" Elizabeth looked stunned. "You can't mean just – just go? Walk off?"

"That's what Ngarana urged us to do. Go. And go now, while you're still alive. That was his message, even if he didn't quite use those words."

"Now, lass," Jim put in mildly. "Let's wait and see. There'll be a lot of hot talk, but I reckon it'll simmer down."

"I don't," Molly said. "And neither do you, if you're honest with yourself."

Jim sat down heavily in the squatter's chair by the window, leaning back in the canvas seat that was like a small hammock. He clasped his hands around one knee and looked about the room.

"I want *you* to go, lass," he said quietly. "Pack some clothes and go into town with Robert and Elizabeth. I'd not like you to spend another night here, just in case. But we built this house and we made this farm out of nothing, and I don't intend to let any man, black or white, drive me out by threats. I'm terribly sorry Birindjie died. But it wasn't my fault, and I don't feel guilty. They'll be angry and sad – Woyongo the chief especially, since he was Birindjie's father. But they'll cool down and get around to seeing it my way, especially when they see I don't intend to run away. They respect a man who stands his ground."

Molly shook her head in distress. "You're the stubbornest man I ever met, Jim Burton! And how could I go and leave you? If you stay, I stay!"

"Suppose," Robert suggested, "you both come back to

Gympie with us, and then in a week or two when things have calmed down, come back and try talking to the aborigines?"

Jim shook his head. "In their present mood they'd burn every building on the place if I left them to their own devices. Molly will go back with you."

"Molly will not!" she declared vigorously.

Jim looked at her with a little smile. "I married a right good lass. But we'll talk about it after lunch. Elizabeth and Robert must be famished, to say nothing of the little lady."

He sat up and held out his arms to Sarah who, aware that something in the strange world of adults was wrong but unable to grasp what it was all about, had been sitting quietly beside Elizabeth. She jumped up at Jim's gesture and went to him and climbed on his knee, because he was a great favourite of hers.

He at once began asking about Sandy, and the conversation generally became more cheerful, and if the threat was not forgotten it was at least for the moment ignored.

After lunch Jim said he wanted to go down to the stables to check a mare about to foal. Robert said casually he'd go too, but Sarah, struck by a sudden thought, wriggled off her chair and caught his hand.

"Daddy, I want to show you something beautiful. It'll only take a minute."

He grinned. "All right, princess. Go ahead," he added to Jim. "I'll be right down as soon as I see something beautiful. Where is it?" he asked Sarah gravely.

"Out here, in the garden," Sarah said importantly, and led him out.

Elizabeth and Molly, watching as they gathered up the lunch dishes and washed them in a tin dish on the table, smiled.

"What do you suppose has struck her so that she remembers and wants him to see?" Molly wondered.

"I think I can guess," Elizabeth said.

Sarah took him straight to the corner of Molly's garden where the roses grew. Never for a moment did it occur to her that the roses might not be in bloom; and one bush kept faith with her. She paused in front of it.

"There. Isn't that the beautifullest thing you ever saw? It's called a rose."

Robert looked down at the crimson petals and then at his daughter's rapt face, and his fingers tightened on her hand.

"Mother had seen one," Sarah was saying, oblivious of the look in Robert's eyes. "Have you ever seen one, Daddy?"

"I believe I have, princess," he said quietly. "A long time ago. But never one so beautiful."

"One day when we have a real house," Sarah went on, "can we have a rose bush?"

"You shall have a real house and a whole garden full of roses, princess, one day. We —"

He spun around. Down near the horse-yard a bursting chorus of wild yells ripped through the afternoon heat.

A party of about a dozen black men exploded from the cover of a clump of trees beyond the barn and, spears at the ready fitted into their womeras – the throwing-sticks which gave the spears so much increased distance and accuracy – ran toward Jim as he walked toward the stables.

"Sarah, go into the house. Run!" Robert ordered as he vaulted over the garden fence and raced toward the pepperina tree where he had tethered the borrowed horse beside the sulky.

When they had left town that morning he had put his rifle on the floor of the sulky, saying he might get a shot at a scrub-turkey.

Elizabeth and Molly burst out of the house together, Elizabeth to snatch up Sarah, Molly to run toward Jim.

"Molly! Get back!" Robert's order came like a whip-crack and instinctively she paused at the command in his voice.

"Get inside!" He had the rifle and was running back toward the corner of the garden. "You'll get in my line of fire."

Both women moved back toward the house, unable to take horror-filled eyes off the scene not two hundred yards away.

Jim had halted and stood perfectly still, facing his attackers as they bore down on him. He seemed to be talking, holding out empty hands, calling something to them, but they took no notice.

A few yards from Jim the grey-haired man who led them checked his stride for a moment, and Jim called: "Woyongo! Listen!"

The old man raised his right arm and hurled his spear.

Clutching his chest, Jim staggered back and fell, and in the same instant Robert, kneeling and steadying the rifle against a fence post, fired. And again, and again.

One black man, in the act of throwing his spear, dropped it and cried out, clutching his leg. As the other bullets struck the ground in front of them, savagely kicking up dust, the charging warriors stopped.

They hesitated, looking at Jim's body, sprawled and still. Then as two more bullets spat dust and whined viciously off stones around them, they broke and fled, the one who had been grazed in the thigh limping but keeping close to the rest.

Robert leapt up, reloading as he ran, and fired twice more after the execution party. Molly was beside him as he reached Jim, and Elizabeth only a few paces behind.

The spear, thrown with the strength of hate, had hit Jim with such force the head had passed right through his shoulder just under the collar bone. Blood was sodden in his shirt and spreading on the grass under him.

Robert's fingers closed over his wrist, and in a moment he looked up at Molly.

"He's alive. Thank God it hit so high. We've got to get that damned spear out. I can cut the head off and pull the shaft, but cutting it won't be easy. They bake the wooden shafts over a fire till they're hard as Lord knows what, and they glue the heads on with something awfully tough."

He pushed the rifle into Elizabeth's hands. "Watch for them. I don't think they'll come back, but if they do, shoot to kill."

He pulled out his pocket knife and said to Molly, "Try to hold the shaft steady."

Feverishly he carved into the wood of the shaft till he could snap off the head that had been so patiently shaped from a piece of flint.

As he took a grip on the shaft to pull it out, Jim's eyes flickered open and he tried to sit up.

"Where are they?" he whispered. "Why didn't they kill me?"

"I interrupted," Robert said. "And I wish you'd stayed unconscious a minute longer. I've got to pull this thing out and it's going to hurt like hell."

Jim made a rueful face. "Hurts like hell now. Get it out, man – just get hold of it and get it out."

Robert nodded. "Hold him," he said to Molly.

She knelt behind Jim, her arms tightly around him, his head against her breast. She was dead white and she hadn't spoken since Jim had been hit, but her hands were steady and her movements controlled.

Jim gasped in pain as Robert pulled the spear out, and

he slid back into unconsciousness again as Molly wiped sweat from his face. Robert swiftly got Jim's shirt off and, pulling off his own, held it wadded tightly against the wound to steady the flow of blood.

"We must carry him up to the house," he said. "Take his feet, Molly. Elizabeth, keep watch for those aborigines. They could come from any direction."

Silently they carried Jim to the house and laid him carefully on the bed while Sarah, wide-eyed with fright, kept quietly in the background. Elizabeth, rifle still in her hands, kept watch from the back door.

Molly tore a sheet into strips to use for bandages. Only when Robert seemed to have succeeded in staunching the flow of blood, she spoke for the first time since the attack.

"Why didn't you kill them?" she demanded fiercely. "You're a soldier and you're a fine shot, I've heard. Why didn't you kill them?"

"This is a pay-back attack," Robert answered levelly. "If I'd killed any more, there'd have to be another attack. A life for a life. Don't think I wasn't tempted. We'll have to get him to a doctor," he added.

"No."

Jim's eyes opened and he spoke the word with strength and finality.

Molly caught his hand. "Jim?"

He smiled crookedly. "I'm all right, lass. But no doctor."

"I'm afraid we've no choice, old chap," Robert told him. "That's a nasty wound and you need help I can't give you. We'll put a mattress on the floor of your buggy – it'll be more comfortable than the sulky I borrowed."

Jim's eyes met Robert's squarely. "Am I dying?"

"I don't think so."

"Then I'm not going near any doctor."

Robert's eyes narrowed. "Now you listen to me. I said I

didn't think you were dying. But without treatment you probably *will* die. And I mean it."

"The man's talking nonsense," Molly told Robert. "I'll get some things packed and we'll take him to a doctor as fast as we can get there."

"No!" Jim tried to sit up, desperation in his eyes. "Don't you see?" he begged, looking from one to the other.

Elizabeth, anxious at the sound of raised voices, had come to the bedroom door. "See what?" she asked.

"Don't you realise what will happen if the word gets out that the blacks tried to kill a white settler? The group will be hunted down and massacred, or the water will be poisoned, or they'll be given gifts of poisoned food. To teach them a lesson. It's all happened before."

Molly stared at him, anger and distress in her face. "Damn them! They deserve it."

"No!"

Sweat was trickling down Jim's face and Robert sponged it away. Then he went over and took the rifle from Elizabeth and stood by the window where he could look down toward the river.

"Don't you see?" Jim asked again. "They have laws, too. They were keeping one of the most fundamental. As they see it, I killed Birindjie because I set him to cut down that tree. Woyongo was within his rights, by their law, to demand my life in payment of his son's. It's a law that is centuries old. I'll not have them murdered for it just because it's not our law."

"That's sheer rubbish, Jim Burton!" Molly cried. "That's the law of savages! I'll not hold my tongue over it."

"We will all hold our tongues over it."

Robert spoke quietly but his voice was as hard as the flint that had made Woyongo's spear-head.

"Robert!"

They were all staring at him, but it was Molly who spoke. "You're not suggesting Jim's right? That these people should go unpunished?"

"I am." He was standing with his back to the room, looking out over the paddocks. "I understand perfectly what Jim means. And I understand perfectly why Woyongo wanted to kill him."

He ran one finger along the rifle barrel as if polishing it. "You see, I lost a son, too. And I hated the man responsible – enough to kill him."

There was a long, still silence. Elizabeth half-stepped toward him and then stopped.

"I don't imagine," Robert went on in the same quiet tone, "that people feel grief, or anger, or love, any less because their skins are black. And so," he added to the silent room, "no one will speak a word of what happened here today. Jim was riding and the horse stumbled and threw him, and a sharp stake drove into his shoulder."

Jim nodded. "That's right. That's what happened, or I don't go to a doctor. That's what happened, even if I die. Promise?"

Molly turned her eyes slowly from Robert to her husband. At last she nodded. "I'm not usually a vengeful person. It's – it was just – everything –" Her voice broke and Jim reached out his good hand and took hers.

"I know, lass. But we still have each other."

An hour later they left Oak Bend.

They made a bed for Jim on the floor of the Burton's buggy and Molly drove their handsome pair of greys while Elizabeth held a parasol over Jim to try to shield him from the summer son. Jim's shotgun, loaded, was at her feet and Robert, as he drove the borrowed sulky with Sarah beside him, had his rifle close under his hand.

They had carried Jim out to the buggy completely covered with a sheet, in the hope that any watching dark eyes might conclude he was dead, thus fulfilling the payback law's demand. But the track led through close bush for much of the way into town, and they couldn't be sure there would not be another attack.

Robert had taken all the horses from the stables, loading the new-born foal into the sulky with the mare watching, so that now she trotted anxiously behind. The other horses he had hastily hitched together, and tied the lead one to the back of the sulky. He had given Sarah a hatchet and said matter-of-factly:

"Princess, if the horses tied to the back get frightened and start pulling the sulky about, or if the black men come to fight us, chop through that first horse's reins to let them all loose. All right?"

And Sarah had nodded understanding.

While Robert had been attending to the horses and making sure no cattle were shut in the yards away from water, the women had swiftly packed the most necessary items which could be transported. They worked quickly, almost without speaking.

Elizabeth, numb with shock at the thought of what was happening, could only guess at the anguish Jim and Molly must be suffering. In what had been open grassland and virgin bush, they had built a comfortable home; they had erected barns and stables and fences. They had ploughed the soil and planted crops. Their cattle grazed the hills and the rich river flats.

To Elizabeth, they had been the personification of security, the living examples of the kind of life she would love.

Security!

She raised her head to look at the homestead as Molly

prepared to climb up into the buggy and take the reins.

Two pepperinas and a willow, graceful in its trailing summer foliage, shaded the house. Down by the barn, hens clucked and scratched in the earth. No one would gather their eggs tomorrow.

Molly, seeing her look, turned also and for a moment stood very still. Then she went to the garden fence, leaned over and plucked the perfect crimson bloom from the rosebush. She went to the sulky and handed the rose to Sarah, then came back very quickly, climbed up and took the reins and drove away, white-faced and silent.

"Lass," Jim began gently, but she shook her head.

"We do what we have to do," she said. "I'll not cry over it. We've a bad journey to make before dark, and I've a sick husband who thank God is nevertheless alive. That's enough to think on. Crying for Oak Bend can wait till later."

Elizabeth looked at Jim, his face drawn with pain and shock.

"Perhaps one day you'll be able to come back."

Her eyes begged him to say yes, not to let her own dreams crumble in the face of the realization that security was a myth.

He closed his eyes and moved his head in a negative gesture.

"It would be suicide," he said. "Someone else can come, some time. If there's anything left to come to. We can maybe sell it, in time. But we can't come back. Not ever."

Twelve

There was no attack on the little cavalcade that made its way through the bush.

But the jolting miles and the heat took toll of Jim's strength so that by the time they arrived in Gympie he was ill indeed.

If the doctor doubted the truth of the story of falling on a sharp stake, he said nothing. Various people asked curious questions about the deserting of Oak Bend, and bringing all the horses, but Molly pointed out with conviction that Jim might never again be able to work as he had previously worked. "And as long as foolish men chase gold he'll never get anyone worth anything to come and work for him," she said reasonably.

And so the story, if not entirely believed, came to be accepted.

After a few days of waiting until the doctor was sure Jim would live, Robert again began to talk of leaving.

"There's nothing to stay for," he said.

It had been raining hard for several days – the start of the wet season – and Elizabeth, looking at the dreariness of slab huts and mud, was forced to agree.

"When do you want to go?"

"I thought perhaps Thursday. It depends. There's a

coach due in from Maryborough tomorrow. I want to ask the driver about going back with him on Thursday. He may know, too, if there are any coastal boats in due to sail south soon."

"Thursday!"

Three days away. Three days to make a decision.

Or was that just something she told herself? A last false pretence of clinging to convention? Hadn't she already decided? If she had ever had doubts about whether or not Robert had killed Dr Miller, he had ended them that terrible day at Oak Bend when he had upheld Woyongo's right to seek revenge for his son's death. When – no doubt without thinking, or perhaps without caring, that he was confessing to murder – he had said: "I understand. I hated ... enough to kill."

John had been right. There was nothing of worth left between people when trust was gone. And one did not – could not – trust a murderer.

Robert was saying, "Is Thursday too soon?"

She pulled her thoughts together. "No," she said slowly. "It's not too soon."

"Good." He picked up his hat and walked out.

She watched him go out into the rain, walking as if he didn't even know it was raining, and she had a strange and terrible feeling of finality, as if already he had walked away from her for the last time.

And yet perhaps in a way he had gone away from her many months ago.

She must have stood at the door, looking out into the rain, for a long time. She knew who the figure in a streaming black oilskin was long before she could distinguish his features through the driving rain.

John Trent shed his oilskin at the door and stepped

inside to just stand looking at her, his fair hair darkened by the rain, his blue eyes anxious.

"Robert's at the 'Wild Swan'," he said. "I had to see you. Is it true he wants to leave this week?"

She nodded.

"Elizabeth —"

She turned away. "I know. Give me another day." Why am I such a coward? she wondered; why such a hypocrite?

"Tomorrow, I promise, I'll give you my answer." When she turned and faced him she was pale but her eyes met his steadily. "And I'll not go back on my decision, whatever it is."

When John had gone and the rain had eased to a drizzle, Elizabeth put on a cloak and went to fetch Sarah home. Molly and Jim Burton had the best guest room at the "Wild Swan" and, now that Jim was out of danger, they liked to have Sarah come for an hour or two and, since she couldn't play outside in such weather, Sarah enjoyed her visits immensely, especially as both Jim and Molly liked to spoil her outrageously.

Elizabeth slipped into the hotel by the back door, as she always did when she came to visit Maggie Doyle, to avoid going through the saloon. There was no sign of Maggie or any of her housemaids in the kitchen, so Elizabeth started up the stairs to the bedrooms.

As she did so she heard one of the bedroom doors open, and a murmur of low voices as a man and a woman came out. Elizabeth froze with her hand on the balustrade and one foot on the third step.

The voices were Robert's and Maggie Doyle's.

Pressed back against the wall so they wouldn't see her from the landing, she backed silently down the stairs and, slipping into the pantry, pulled the door to.

Closing her eyes in the dimness, she put her hands to her face. Why should I care? she thought. Here I am planning to leave my husband for another man; why should I care if he amuses himself elsewhere? I don't care. Of course I don't care — not that way. Just for the moment it was a jolt to my pride, I suppose; what an ego I have! I should be glad. I suppose I am glad, in a way, that he can find pleasure in another woman, perhaps even really care for her; because it means I can leave him and know it doesn't matter so very much to him. That's why I don't want them to see me: I don't want to spoil anything for him.

They were coming down the stairs, talking less guardedly now.

"You're a funny mixture of a man, aren't you?" Maggie Doyle was saying in her best Cockney.

"Why?" Robert's tone was almost gruff. "I'm almost human, sometimes; that's all."

"Why'd you bother with that old drunk? You don't know him from Adam, I'll bet. He passes out cold in me saloon, having had the foresight to spend every bloomin' penny in his pocket on grog so's he don't have nothin' left to pay for a room, an you pick him up an' put him to bed an' tell me to see he gets breakfast. I'll lay a bet you don't have no spare cash to throw around either, so why'd you bother with him? He's nothin' but a drunken old tramp an' always will be an' you know it. So?"

"I'd had a couple of lucky hands at poker," Robert said lightly.

"Yeah? Strikes me you could use the money yerself instead of givin' beds an' meals to tramps. All right, all right, it's none of me bleedin' business. I just wondered, that's all."

There was a little silence. They had paused at the foot of the stairs.

"You called him a drunken old tramp," Robert said quietly, "and so he is. But you see, Maggie, he's only what I would be without my family. A man has to have some kind of roots, some kind of reason for living. You've seen a lot of humanity, Maggie. You know what the cards would do to me – or the gold-fever, or the horses, or some other gamble. That's the only difference between me and that poor old boy we just carried upstairs: he doesn't have my Elizabeth."

He strode through into the saloon and after a moment Maggie went into the kitchen.

For a long time Elizabeth stood in the darkness of the pantry, her fingers gripped on a shelf as if the spinning darkness in her mind might swallow her if she relaxed her grip on something solid.

Robert.

For a while it was the only word that could surface in her thoughts. Robert needing her. Robert, without her, without the sheet-anchor of his family, sliding down to become a derelict.

Without her, John would survive. John would always survive.

Robert would not.

From that, there was no escape, no freedom.

She opened her eyes in the dimness of the hotel pantry. "I can't leave him," she whispered.

She knew in that moment she must come to grips with, and try to understand, the terrible thing that had driven Robert to kill Abraham Miller – the same deep, primitive instinct which drove Woyongo to order *his* son's death avenged.

Civilization was a very thin veneer, shed all too easily. That was something she had to face, and live with, even if she could never accept it.

She opened the pantry door and went slowly upstairs to fetch Sarah.

By next morning the rain had cleared and the sun was hot and bright, though a breeze tempered the heat. The river was brown and swollen, but the town had almost the air of a cormorant spreading its wings in the sun and breeze to dry, as people came out into the muddy streets and washing flapped from hundreds of clotheslines.

Robert had taken Sarah, accompanied by Sandy, to the "Wild Swan" on her usual afternoon visit to the Burtons, and he walked on to the cabin Bert Peters occupied, to give Bert the news that he was leaving for Victoria.

Bert nodded. "Been thinking of moving out, myself. Might push that old shaft of Doc Miller's and mine another few feet. Haven't touched it for a long time, but I've been thinking of it lately."

He shrugged. "I dunno. You know the way it is. You know it's useless. But some little devil keeps nagging you: what if you went another foot? Or another?"

Robert grinned. "Oh, yes, I know the way it is. But I've explored every possibility in my claim. No sense to take out another. Cut my losses and go."

"How does Mrs Walden feel about moving?"

"She probably has mixed feelings," Robert said, and stood up as he heard a step outside and looked up to see John Trent. "Hello, John. Well, I've got to meet a fellow at two o'clock and it must be getting close to that."

Bert pulled out an ornate gold watch. "Twenty minutes to the hour," he said.

John was staring. "That's Dr Miller's watch!" he said sharply — so sharply that, at the doorway, Robert turned.

"That's right," Bert nodded. "He left it behind him when he was here the day he was —" He stopped and glanced at Robert. "The day of the fire. He come in just before dark and stayed and had a bit of scran – I was just cooking my tea. Then he said he had a couple of calls to make and went off. He'd wound his watch and put it on the table, and he went off and left it. I didn't notice till he'd gone, and I didn't worry because I thought I'd see him next day. But it didn't work out that way."

John said nothing.

Bert looked at him anxiously. "Maybe I should've gave it to the police or someone, but the doc had no relatives, and he and I were partners in the mine. I didn't think anyone would mind. Do you think I done the wrong thing?"

"No," John said slowly. "No, of course not."

"You could say it was the only gold our partnership ever produced," Bert said wryly.

"Yes," John agreed. "I'm sure no one would mind you keeping the watch under those circumstances."

"It's a nice watch, and I never owned one," Bert said a trifle wistfully, "but I wouldn't want to keep it if it *belonged* to anyone – you know, relatives, like. But there's none."

He put the watch away. "You wanted me for something, Mr Trent?" he asked cheerfully.

"Yes." John nodded. "Yes, the new bridle and saddle you were asking about – the new stock came in yesterday. You – ah – buying a horse?"

Bert grinned. "I haven't robbed the gold escort. Yes, I'm thinking of moving on, and for once in my life, what with odd jobs around the town, I've scraped up enough money to buy a horse. Decided I'm too old to be walking the road any more. Thanks, I'll drop around later and have a look. What's the price?"

Robert walked away, a little frown pulling his dark brows together.

Now what the *devil* happened just then? he asked himself.

Old John looked like a stunned mullet; sounded about as bright, too.

He glanced at the sky, noting absently that heavy cloud was rolling up from the south again; looked as though they were still getting rain farther upstream. But most of his mind was focussed on the scene he had just witnessed.

What had happened to make John Trent look like that?

Whatever it was, it had happened when Bert produced Abraham Miller's watch. But there had been a perfectly simple explanation for that, and Bert had been completely unruffled.

Surely not even John could be so blasted straight-laced that he'd regard Bert's action as theft? Surely not! But he'd looked as shocked as if Bert had been guilty of robbing Miller's grave. Why shouldn't Bert keep the old bastard's watch? Good luck to him!

And yet –

Something, some half-formed idea, stirred just below the level of conscious thought, and Robert stepped behind the cover of a parked German waggon and turned to watch Bert's hut.

In less than a minute John came out and walked away. His back was turned to Robert so that he couldn't see John's face. But it was Bert, not John, who riveted his attention.

Bert had come to the door of his shack to say a casual, cheery goodbye to John, but as he stood and watched John walk away there was no cheerfulness in his face.

He watched until John was out of sight, standing utterly motionless, his face dark with some unfathomable expression.

There was something so menacing about it that Robert felt his scalp tingle.

When Bert finally turned and went inside, Robert

slipped out from behind the cover of the waggon and walked slowly away. His mind was racing and he could feel his heart quicken its beat.

"But that's crazy!" he said aloud.

An elderly Chinese, hurrying up from somewhere down by the river, threw him a startled glance and went on. Robert didn't even notice him.

It wasn't possible. Bert and Abraham Miller had been friends – partners, even though their mine had turned out a dud.

Robert stopped in mid-stride.

For a second he stood still, feeling as if someone had punched him in the stomach and knocked all the breath from his body.

Then he set off for Bert's claim at a run.

It was a couple of hundred yards away. At first, Bert had lived on the site in a tent, but when the mine proved worthless he had moved into a deserted shack some distance away and, with his skilled hands, made the shack weatherproof and reasonably comfortable.

With a quick glance around to check that he was unobserved, Robert climbed down the shaft. Half way down he remembered Bert had driven a lateral tunnel, and he would need a light, but after only a moment's hesitation he went on down.

At the bottom of the shaft was mud and slush. He got down on hands and knees and started into the horizontal tunnel. The roof and walls had been carefully shored and, just as the light from the shaft began to fade into the shadow of the tunnel, he found a pick and shovel leaning against the wall, and a tin box with Bert's miner's lamp and lucifers.

Robert lit the lamp and, taking the pick, went on into the damp darkness.

It was a very short distance to the end of the tunnel, and all the light showed was rock, earth and emptiness. There was still rock-rubble heaped against the face of the tunnel's end.

Feeling foolish, he chipped some of the rubble away with the pick.

Presently he slowly lowered the pick and sat back on his heels. Under the piled rock was the white glint of quartz, and the dull gleam of yellow metal.

For a time – he would never know how long – he just sat there, staring. Finally, slowly and carefully, he picked out a nugget the size of a walnut from its surrounding quartz, held it in his hand, wonderingly, for a little while, and then laid it down almost reverently in the tin box where Bert had stored his miner's lamp.

The palms of his hands began to sweat with a wild surge of excitement. He snatched up the pick and swung it at the tunnel-face again and again in a fury of desire. He must gouge more gold, and more, from this treasure-house of wealth, working in a mindless frenzy, uncaring of aching muscles or gasping breath or streaming sweat, unthinking of the fact that he was a trespasser here.

He burned with the fever that demanded he snatch more and more, in a kind of terror that it might all vanish like river-mist. It was the kind of fever that had seized Bert Peters and crazed him with greed – the terrible greed that can be born of sudden wealth, wealth beyond dreams: the greed that feeds on ruthlessness, and grows the more it is fed.

Thirteen

John Trent walked slowly.

He didn't consciously turn toward the Waldens' shack, but he knew that was where he was going. Today, Elizabeth had told him, she would give him her answer.

Last night he hadn't slept – hadn't even bothered to undress because he knew sleep would be impossible. He had sat at the window and watched the day come, and hope had risen in him with the sun, and had shone as brightly through the morning.

He wished he could make her his wife. But did a piece of paper mean all that much? He could give her – and Sarah too – all the consideration Robert would never give. And she would have his utter loyalty, all his life; and his admiration, and his love. He mightn't be very good at saying things like that. But he meant them. He guessed Robert Walden, with his good looks and his gay manner, was very good at saying all those things. But when Robert said them there was no solidarity in them; only charm.

But John wasn't thinking of any of that now.

He walked without seeing anyone around him. Someone spoke to him and he smiled politely, but he didn't hear what was said.

All he could see was a gold watch in Bert Peters' hand. And all he could hear was his own brain, clear and calculating, telling him that now he had a choice.

And John Trent felt he would never face such a terrible choice again if he lived two lifetimes.

If he told Elizabeth what he knew, he was certain that would be enough to tip the scales for her: she would choose to stay with Robert. And if he held his tongue –

He wasn't twenty yards from the Waldens' hut when Elizabeth, in bonnet and gloves, came out. She paused when she saw him.

"John! I was just coming to see you." She stepped back. "Come in."

He took off his hat and dropped it on the table, his eyes on her face, and stepped forward to take her hands. "Elizabeth?"

She was pale and he guessed she had slept no more than he had, but her clear eyes met his steadily.

"I'm sorry, John," she said very quietly.

Neither of them moved for a long minute. Then he closed his eyes and dropped her hands. "I see."

"I must go with Robert," she said. "I thought for a while I had a choice. But I haven't."

"Even though you believe he's a murderer?" he said harshly.

"Even so."

He turned away. "Do you know – really know – what going with him will mean, every day of your life? Always moving on, always debts, always insecurity?"

She bent her head. "I know. Oh, yes, I know that very well. But – he needs me. More than ever, now."

She looked up. "I married him with open eyes, John. I knew what he was like. But I loved him very much and I thought – I thought that would be enough." She smiled very faintly.

"I believe it always was enough, till – till now. It was a

lovely dream you gave me, John: security, and peace, and – safety. But one has to wake from dreams. I'm only sorry – so very sorry – you've been hurt."

There was a long silence.

Then John said: "Ruth."

Elizabeth looked at him. "I beg your pardon?"

"I was thinking of Ruth, in the Bible. Whither thou goest, I will go, and thy people shall be my people."

"Except," Elizabeth said quietly, "that Robert will never have people. Not friends that last, perhaps not even a country, because he's never still long enough. His only people will be Sarah and me. I can't take that from him."

"I guess," John said slowly, "I was thinking of Joseph's brothers, too, selling him for twenty pieces of silver."

She stared. "I'm sorry. I can't think very clearly. What are you talking about?"

He took her arm and put her gently into a chair. Then he sat down heavily opposite her.

"My dear, half an hour ago I learned that Robert did not kill Abraham Miller. And as long as I live I will never know whether or not I'd have told you – or anyone else – if you'd decided to leave him. Oh, my price was a lot higher than twenty pieces of silver. But I still might have sold another man."

She was still staring at him, numbly.

"Not Robert?" It was barely more than a whisper. "Not Robert?"

She leapt up and grabbed his arm wildly, shaking him.

"John! Is that what you said? *It wasn't Robert?*"

He nodded. "It was not Robert."

She turned slowly, hands outstretched like a blind woman, groping for a chair. He sprang forward to catch her as she fainted.

When she came spinningly back to consciousness he had laid her on the bed and taken off her bonnet and gloves and was standing beside her with a tin pannikin of water.

"Drink some," he said.

She obeyed, and sat up, covering her face with shaking hands. Presently she looked up at him, wonderingly.

"But – John, who? And how do you know?"

He smiled. "One thing at a time. First, are you all right?"

"Yes." She touched his arm. "You're so very kind. It was such a foolish thing to do, to faint then. It was just – I still can't feel anything but a kind of numbness. Please, tell me."

"Bert Peters has Dr Miller's watch. I recognized it, and he quite readily admitted it was the doctor's. He says Miller left it at Bert's place when he dropped in for a visit on the evening of the fire. But when I went to Dr Miller's with my broken wrist that night, he took that watch from his pocket and told me it was eleven o'clock and he wasn't seeing anyone. Bert's lying. There's only one way he could have got that watch: he was in Miller's house after midnight. And there's only one explanation for that."

"Bert!" Elizabeth looked bewildered. "But why? Surely – surely no one kills to steal a watch!"

John shook his head. "I don't know. I can't think too well at the moment."

"Bert! So kind, so casual, never asking anything from life but the pleasure of living it! To kill for petty theft?"

"Maybe it wasn't the watch. Maybe there was something else – a quarrel of some kind, and Bert hit him and killed him, and then saw the watch and couldn't resist the temptation to take it."

"They said Dr Miller was struck from behind," Elizabeth said. "That doesn't sound like a blow struck in quick anger, such as might happen in a quarrel. It means he was hit when he wasn't looking – perhaps even while he was asleep. It sounds like something –" She shivered. "It sounds like something terribly deliberate."

"I know. I can't guess the reasons. I only know Bert Peters did kill Miller. He must have."

"What will you do?"

He ran a hand through his fair hair. "I haven't thought that far. Tell Robert, first. After that —"

He paused. "Elizabeth, I don't know that going to the authorities would do much good. Bert has a perfectly good story about the watch. It's one man's word against another's. That wouldn't stand up in a court of law and the police would know they couldn't act on it."

He stood up.

"I must go. I must find Robert, and tell him."

Elizabeth held out her hand. "John —"

He put a finger gently on her lips, and shook his head. He stooped and kissed her forehead and then turned quickly away and went out, walking rapidly.

He walked toward his store, eyes on the ground but not noticing the mud that caked his boots as he strode without caring where his feet went.

Some part of his mind registered the fact that there was a great deal of activity in the town, but he didn't think about it.

Someone called to him: "You'll be glad your place is up the hill, Mr Trent."

He nodded automatically, "Yes, indeed."

He had gone another ten paces before the remark and his own reply penetrated his numbness. He stopped and looked around him, puzzled.

Everywhere people were hurrying. People on foot, people in any kind of horse-drawn conveyance; and all carried things — all manner of things: tools, bundles of clothes, blankets, household possessions.

He stood gaping for several seconds, jostled by passersby, unable to bring his mind to focus on what was happening. A man he didn't know said, "Gawd, they must've had some rain upstream. They say the One Mile's going under."

John looked, then, at the river.

Brown, racing, filled with cedar logs and all manner of debris, it was a thing gone mad, spilling out over the low-lying land, into houses and stores and hotels.

He ran down toward the edge of the flood and watched the water-level against a post. In two minutes he had his answer: it was still rising, and rising fast.

Staring at the water, he backed away from it, almost as if it were a live creature risen from some prehistoric nightmare to threaten him. There was a small depression between the Waldens' hut and higher ground. Very soon, Elizabeth could be cut off, caught between the river and a breakaway arm of floodwater.

He raced back toward the shack. Already the water had broken over and was running shallowly through the depression. He splashed through it and pounded on the door of the shack.

"The river!" he said in answer to Elizabeth's startled look. "Pack some things quickly, I've got to get you out of here or we'll be cut off. It's rising like a mad thing. Where's Sarah? And the dog?"

"Both at the 'Wild Swan' with the Burtons. John —"

"Thank God. She'll be all right there. Get some clothes, blankets – anything you value that we can carry. Quickly."

"John, where's Robert?"

"I don't know." He was pulling blankets from beds and rolling them together. "He said he was going to meet someone at two o'clock."

"That's hours ago!" Elizabeth looked up anxiously in her hasty packing of clothes into a valise.

"Robert will be all right. He's quite able to look after himself." He didn't notice her small, wistful smile. "Have you any valuables – money, jewellery?"

"No jewellery. There's a little money I – we have hidden for safekeeping."

She moved a loose stone in the chimney corner and took out a small leather purse. He watched her without comment. Not even to him would she admit that, in order to survive, she had to hide money from Robert.

"Bert built that fireplace," she said, and went on with the packing.

John looked out. "We have to go, Elizabeth, or it won't be safe to cross the gully."

"Books!" she cried. "We must have the books!"

"They're too heavy," he told her practically, "and there isn't time."

"Just two or three. We must have books." She ran her hands over the backs of the volumes that stood on a wooden shelf Robert had made from a packing-case, and pulled out three.

John caught her arm. "Come."

Outside it was growing dusk prematurely because of the heavy cloud, though it still was not raining. It was the torrential rain which had fallen a day and a half ago on the ranges where the river rose, which was sending it rampaging now.

"Hold on to me," John ordered as they waded into the water that raced, waist-deep now, through the gully that lay between them and high ground. Holding the valise with one hand, trying to keep it clear of the water, Elizabeth clutched John's arm to steady herself, feeling with her feet for secure footing in the tugging water.

Someone said, "Give me your hand," and she looked up

to see with relief a man standing on the far bank, reaching out to help her. He came into the water up to his knees and took her hand as she held it out to him.

"Thank you," she said.

And it was only then, in the anxiety and the uncertain light of early dusk that she saw the man was Bert Peters.

She gasped in shock and his fingers tightened on her wrist as in one swift movement he pulled her backwards against him, and in his other hand held a butcher's knife at her throat.

"You'll do whatever I say, Trent," Bert said flatly. "Or I'll kill her in front of your eyes."

Fourteen

Robert climbed slowly out of the shaft.

He had no idea how long he had been down there, but he was surprised to find how dusk had begun to close in. He wiped his sweat-and-dust-grimed face and flexed tired muscles, reflecting that perhaps only exhaustion had, in the end, pulled him back to his senses and made him think. And now he had scant thought for the little pile of gold-filled quartz he had left on the floor of the shaft.

He went quickly to Bert Peters' hut. The door was standing open and the hut was empty. For a moment he stood frowning, and then set off for John Trent's store almost at a run.

It was a while before he noticed that everyone seemed to be hurrying, and odd phrases reached him: "Can't believe it"; "so fast"; "water lapping"; "It's in Curnows' "; "road's flooded".

At Trent's General Store an aproned clerk told him: "We haven't seen Mr Trent since lunch-time, Captain Walden. He's probably helping people move out of the low-lying parts."

"Oh. The river's in flood, is it?"

The clerk looked at him in astonishment. "I'll *say* it is!"

Robert thanked him and went out. I know, he reflected grimly, where John Trent has gone.

He walked down Mary Street and then veered away toward his own shack, going more slowly now, head down, hands in his pockets. He was about to face the truth, he realized, about several things; he was not altogether sure he wanted to know what the truth was.

When he came in sight of the river he looked at it idly, and stopped short in disbelief. Then he plunged down the hill toward the shack. There were hardly any people around here, now. They had all moved themselves and whatever belongings they could to higher ground.

Three people were standing on the bank of the gully which was normally dry and which was now three feet deep in swirling water. Even in the fading light he could see the woman was Elizabeth and he guessed one of the men would be John Trent.

Robert stopped as suddenly as if he had walked into a glass wall. He could see now who the third man was, and he could see exactly what he meant to do with his prisoners.

The situation was perfect for Bert.

The flooded river churned the racing cedar logs, the remains of the masses the timbergetters had put into the river to be rafted down to Maryborough and the coastal trade. It would be very simple – since in the circumstances John could be made to do anything he was told – for Bert to hit him with something to knock him out while his attention was distracted. Elizabeth, in her long, sodden skirt, could never get away from Bert even if he released her for a few moments. Two bodies – even if they were ever found – would go down as victims of the flood, swept away while trying to escape from low ground. Any injuries on the bodies would be put down to debris in the river. The situation was perfect, and Bert had seized it boldly.

Without either haste or stealth, Robert walked toward them.

Elizabeth could feel the edge of the blade against her throat as Bert Peters kept her right arm twisted painfully behind her in a vicious grip. She wished desperately that she had told John she had put Robert's rifle in the roll of blankets; though even as she thought of it she realized that long before John could undo the bundle and get the rifle Bert could kill them both.

"Now then," Bert snapped, "let's go. You lead the way, Trent. And if you try anything Mrs Walden will be dead before you can turn around. We'll walk around the edge of the river till we're behind them trees, though it's getting too dark for anybody to see too much, anyway."

John looked at Bert. "Let her go," he said steadily. "I'm the one you want, not Mrs Walden. She knows nothing about it."

Bert laughed. "D'you think I'm daft? She knows, all right. You're solid bone between the ears if you think I don't know that the first thing you'd do is tell her. Now move."

John's anguished eyes met Elizabeth's. "My dear —"

"It's all right, John," she said. "It's not your fault. We haven't any choice but to do as he says."

"There's someone coming!" Bert said sharply. "He'd best toe the line." He pressed the knife a fraction harder against Elizabeth's throat.

She knew, even in the dim light, the easy walk of the newcomer, and she wanted to scream a warning, but the pressure of the blade kept her silent. She knew the edge had cut her skin shallowly, because she could feel a tiny trickle of blood down her neck. They all stood motionless, waiting.

"Well, well, well," Robert said. "An interesting little group. Have we all been introduced?"

"Don't try being funny," Bert said roughly. "You'll do as you're told or I'll cut your wife's throat."

Robert thrust his hands into his trouser-pockets and laughed. "My dear chap, do so by all means," he said.

For a moment there was no sound but the dull roar of the river. The little group might have been painted figures on canvas, some surrealist's depiction of shock.

"What're you playing at?" Bert demanded.

Robert shook his head. "I'm not playing, I assure you. If you want to kill her, go ahead. You're just saving me the trouble."

"Robert!" It was John who found bewildered voice. "For God's sake, what are you saying? It's your wife!"

Robert looked at Elizabeth and his eyes were hard as ice.

"Oh, yes," he said. "My wife. My loyal and loving wife who was perfectly happy to leave me for someone with a little more in the way of hard cash. You didn't know that, Bert, did you?"

He jerked his head towards John. "They were going off together. So they thought. But I'm not the kind of man you play those games with. That surprises you, my dear, doesn't it?" He looked at Elizabeth. "You thought I'd be the gentleman and let you go? Oh, no. If I can't have you, no one does."

Elizabeth, her face ashen, whispered, "Robert," but the word was drowned in the river's snarling.

"I'd have attended to this chore earlier," Robert went on, "but I was busy. I took the liberty of going down your shaft, Bert. I had an interesting afternoon."

"You bastard!" Bert shouted. "What are you *playing* at?"

"*There's* a tidbit of gossip for you," Robert said conversationally to John Trent. "The reason Bert killed off Dr Miller: that mine is no schicer, believe me. There's a nice lot of gold in there, and I suspect quite a nice lot has come out. But Bert didn't run up any little red flag, and he didn't tell the doctor, either. Because he wasn't satisfied with half the mine, were you, Bert? Oh, no. He wanted it all. I don't blame him. In fact, I understand perfectly how he felt. For a little while this afternoon I wanted it all for myself, too."

"I never had nothing," Bert muttered. "Never. And what good would it have done the doc? Just bought him a few more bottles of brandy. I tried to buy out his share of the mine, but the old fool thought it was a joke to have a share in a dud claim. A joke!"

He sneered. "And you set yourself up to take the drop for me if anything went wrong, and they found out Miller's death wasn't an accident. You made your threats and you let me get you drunk. I'd have killed Miller anyway, but you took all the risk out of it for me." He laughed. "He said he wouldn't let me in, that night when I knocked on his door. So I told him I'd struck gold. He opened the door fast enough then!"

"I remember," Robert said, "that you mentioned to me this afternoon that you were going to have one last go at the claim before you left town. I imagine you've told several people that, haven't you? And – presto! You will bound up that shaft one day, all elated, and announce to the world you've struck gold."

"That's right," Bert said. "No one's to know the gold I've already taken out wasn't found that one day. I don't have to hide nothing. But I had to wait, after the doc died. I had to wait a long while so's no one'd ever guess."

He looked at Robert with hatred. "What are you going to do?"

"When I've recovered from the shock of my poor wife's death in the flooded river – and that of the family friend who gallantly tried to rescue her, of course," he added with a little bow to John Trent, "I think you and I might go into partnership, Bert."

"You *fool*, Robert!" John flung at him bitterly. "You stupid *fool*! She wasn't going to leave you. Do you hear me? I wanted her to – oh, yes. But she wouldn't leave you. Why else do you think I was so blind and deaf I didn't know the river was rising? Why else do you think I was so damned stupid I didn't stop to think that Peters might come after me? She wouldn't leave you! Even though she thought –"

He stopped.

"Even though she thought I was a murderer?" Robert finished for him. "How touching. Nice try, John. Quite the gentleman, aren't you? Elizabeth showed good taste in choosing you, I will admit. Unfortunately, I'm not such a fool as to believe you."

Almost casually he stepped up to John and crashed his fist into John's midriff. As he doubled up, Robert hit him a neat, downward-chopping blow with the heel of his hand at the base of the skull. John pitched forward and lay still, face down in the mud.

Robert rubbed his hand. "A method of approach useful in many a barrack-room brawl," he said. "Roll him into the river, Bert, while I have the pleasure of attending to the lady."

"Stay away!" Bert snapped. "I'll do it myself."

"Then you'd better turn the knife the right way around," Robert advised. "That's the back of it you're using."

Instinctively Bert looked down, and drew the knife away six inches to see the blade.

Like a striking snake Robert leapt and, grabbing Bert's wrist with both hands, forced his arm out and up so sharply that Bert with a yell of fury let Elizabeth go in order to swing a punch at Robert's head with his free hand.

"Elizabeth! Run!" Robert shouted. "For God's sake, run! I might not be able to hold him."

His hands locked on Bert's wrist, he fought to twist it to force loose the bigger man's grasp on the knife. Bert crashed his left fist again and again in restricted jabs into the side of Robert's head, at the same time thrusting forward with the full weight of his body in an effort to bring Robert down.

In the end his superior weight won and the two men went down in the mud, with Robert underneath, and Bert still holding the knife. Robert still had his grip on Bert's wrist but he knew now that he couldn't maintain it, because with no free hand he couldn't defend himself against the rain of blows Bert was bringing down on him.

Somehow he had to get free of Bert's weight on him, of Bert's knee jammed crushingly into his stomach, forcing the breath from his body. He would have to break free, let Bert's knife-hand go, and take a chance on finding, perhaps, a piece of wood or some similar object to use for a weapon.

Time. That was what he needed. He had to give Elizabeth time to get to safety. How far would she have got by now? He had no idea how long this fight had been going on, but he did know that pretty soon Bert was going to batter him insensible enough to let go that knife-hand.

He bunched his muscles for one desperate effort to get clear.

And Elizabeth's voice said clearly, "Drop that knife, Bert, or I'll blow your head off."

For a fraction of a second Robert thought he was hallucinating under Bert's head-punches. Then he realized Bert had gone very still.

"You can let his arm go now, Robert," Elizabeth said in the same level tone. "Get up, Bert. With your hands over your head."

Bert obeyed, his jaw slack with shock.

His ears singing with semi-consciousness, Robert sat up. The knife was lying in the mud and he picked it up and got slowly to his feet.

Elizabeth was holding his Remington rifle levelled coldly at Bert Peters.

"Where'd you get that?" Bert demanded hoarsely.

"I packed it in the blanket-roll John was doing up. Now you will walk, slowly and with your hands up, into town and up to the police station."

Bert backed away, his eyes wild.

"No," he said. "No! No!" His voice rose in a scream of rage.

He wheeled and ran into the river, splashing through the shallows, wading deeper.

"Let him go," Robert told Elizabeth.

As the swirling brown water came up around his armpits, Bert struck out, swimming powerfully, skilfully using the current.

"Let him go," Robert said again, watching as if mesmerized.

Even in the deepening dusk they could see that in forty yards he was in difficulties, faltering, all the strength gone from his swimming. He turned and, instead of making for the far bank, tried to get back. But he was floundering and helpless, and in a few strokes he went under.

Elizaberh put down the rifle and turned slowly, her hands outstretched as if feeling for something to hold on to.

"Robert," she whispered.

He caught her against him and held her tightly, his face against her hair.

"Oh, God," he said. "Oh, God." He went on holding her wordlessly until the violent shivering that shook her body stopped.

"Oh, my Elizabeth," he said softly. "I've never been so afraid as when I saw Bert had you with that damned knife – I couldn't creep on him, I couldn't rush him. I had to try to make him think I might be on his side, had to try to make him unsure. I had to say – all those things." His arms tightened around her. "Oh, Elizabeth."

She took a long breath and looked up at him, and touched his swollen cheek.

"It was true, Robert. What John said. I wasn't going to leave you."

He kissed her very gently. "I wouldn't have blamed you if you had."

She moved suddenly in his arms. "John!" she cried anxiously.

"He's all right. He'll have a most frightful headache when he comes to, but he's all right. I had to knock him out to try to make Bert believe that ugly charade." He smiled a little crooked smile. "And I'm afraid I wanted to hit him, anyway."

"How long have you known?" Elizabeth asked.

"That John was in love with you? Oh, I don't know. I'm not blind, or even quite that stupid. I had to let you make your own decision, or nothing meant anything. So I had to hold my tongue."

"He would never have asked me to leave you," she said urgently, "if he hadn't –"

She stopped.

"If he hadn't believed I was a murderer, and known you believed it, too," Robert said. "No, I don't think he would."

"Robert –"

He kissed her quickly. "I know. I know you didn't want to believe it; but what else could you think? What else could anyone think? It was partly true, in a way. Because I *wanted* to kill Miller. Poor drunken devil. I wanted so much to kill him I was constantly afraid I might."

She lifted her head sharply. "That's – *that's* what you meant? The day Jim was attacked by the aborigines. You said – you hated Dr Miller enough to kill him."

His arms tightened around her again. "And you thought I meant I had killed him? I'm sorry. I didn't mean to do that to you."

He held her a little away from him and looked down at her gravely.

"There's something else you should know about me. I'll never know, the rest of my life, whether I'd have tried to save John tonight if you hadn't been in danger, too. Because you see, all I had to do was mind my own business, and the danger of losing you to John Trent was over. I knew Bert would be out to kill him."

She met his eyes steadily. "You'd have tried to save him."

"I'm not," Robert said, "so sure."

There was a little silence. Elizabeth shook her head dazedly. "Bert. I still don't think I've quite absorbed it. Even –" She put her hand to her throat and shivered.

"Think how kind he was to Sarah over the dog. He was a man who never cared about money. Then to kill for it –"

"He never cared when he had nothing. Then when he found gold – That's what gold can do," he said slowly and soberly. "I know that. For a few hours in that shaft this afternoon I was a madman, blind and deaf and insensible to everything but the gold. I forgot that Bert would go after John. Forgot John would go to you, and might lead Bert there. I –"

John Trent groaned and tried to sit up. They went to him.

"It's all right, John," Robert said. "Just sit there for a while till you feel better."

John was shaking his head, trying to clear his vision. "Elizabeth –"

"I'm here, John. I'm all right."

He stared. "Peters! Where –"

"He's dead," Robert said, and somehow the flat matter-of-factness of his tone was a clear indication of the fear they had all felt. "He tried to get away by swimming the river. He didn't make it."

Elizabeth looked at the river and then at Robert. "Do you suppose he was hit by a log or something? It looked – as if he was dragged down –" There was horror in her voice.

"I think he *was* dragged down," Robert said grimly. "I think he was carrying gold – quite a lot of it. While we were fighting I felt something hard under his shirt. I think he had gold – probably in some kind of belt – fastened to him for safekeeping. When he tried to get away he forgot it – forgot how it would weigh him down, and in that current –"

He paused. "That's why I told you to let him go. Better to let him kill himself."

"I couldn't have shot him," Elizabeth said simply.

Robert put his arm around her shoulders. "No," he said. "I guess not, when he was running away."

"I couldn't have shot him at any time," she said. "I packed the rifle in the roll of blankets, but I forgot to bring any ammunition. That was an empty gun I was holding at his head."

Robert stared at her and then flung his head back and laughed. "Oh, what a girl I married," he said.

Then he was quickly serious. "Elizabeth, I *will* win, one day. My luck will change. You'll have all the things you want."

She bent her head for a moment, and when she looked up she smiled. "Of course," she said.

John Trent got shakily to his feet. "I wish," he said, "someone would tell me what's been happening here. Or did I just have a nightmare?"

"Come," Robert said. "We're all of us a bit shaky. We'd better get into town or it'll be so dark we'll all fall down a mine shaft. I think we'll try Maggie's place. I've a feeling she might be a good nurse."

The "Wild Swan", like every sizeable building above flood-level, was jammed with people who had fled from the rampaging river.

Maggie Doyle had taken one look at the drenched and muddied trio and had taken them upstairs to her private sitting-room, where she plied them with brandy and gave orders for hot water to be brought up. She sent someone to fetch a change of clothes for John and took Elizabeth into her own bedroom to wash and change.

"I must go and tell the Burtons and Sarah you're safe," Maggie said. "They've been worried stiff. Even Sandy's looking disconsolate."

She asked only one question, of Elizabeth.

"Is it safe to leave those two men together? They've been fighting."

Elizabeth smiled. "Quite safe. They haven't been fighting each other. Or not exactly."

When Elizabeth came back into the sitting-room, John was lying on the sofa, looking in bewilderment at the room and its contents, and Maggie was carefully bathing Robert's battered face.

"You may feel just as sick tomorrow as he will, luv," she was saying to John, "but he ain't half going to look more spectacular."

She looked up as Elizabeth came in, and smiled, and Elizabeth thought she had never seen Margaret Doyle look so gay. Why, Elizabeth thought, she's a beautiful woman; or does she look that way to me because life itself looks more beautiful when you've almost lost it?

"Had quite a day, I believe," Maggie said. "Well, it's over now and I'll get some food sent up to you while I find some beds. Lord luv a duck, the place is swarming with people tonight."

John sat up. "No. Thank you, Mrs Doyle, but I must go. There'll be people needing things from the store, and maybe some will need to sleep in the building – it'd hold quite a number. I must see what I can do to help."

He said goodnight quickly to Robert and Elizabeth. Robert shook hands and Elizabeth reached up to kiss his cheek, then turned and tucked her arm through Robert's.

Maggie walked downstairs with John.

At the door she touched his arm. "She'll be all right," she said.

John shook his head. "He'll destroy her."

"Oh, no," she said quietly. "It's from him she draws her strength."

"From him?" John said incredulously. "He's the weak one! If it weren't for her –"

"Exactly. He needs her. And a woman like Elizabeth needs to be needed."

His hand on the door, John suddenly swung around. "How did you know?" he demanded.

"About you and Elizabeth Walden? Let's just say that in my line of business one learns a great deal about human nature."

He was staring at her as if he had never seen her before in his life.

"You – your voice!" he said. "It's different. You're not speaking like a Cockney at all!"

"Wasn't I? I must have forgotten for a moment." She smiled. "Let's leave it till another day, shall we?"